South Carolina
State Facts

Nickname:	Palmetto State
Date Entered Union:	May 23, 1788 (the 8th state)
Motto:	*Animis opibusque parati/Dum spiro spero* (Prepared in mind and deed/While I breathe, I hope)
South Carolina Men:	Dizzy Gillespie, *jazz trumpeter* Jesse Jackson, *civil rights leader* Joe Frazier, *prize fighter* Ronald McNair, *astronaut*
State Tree:	Palmetto
State Bird:	Carolina wren
Fun Fact:	The state dance of South Carolina is the Shag.

S0-AGF-665

Was nudity subtle? Hardly!

Persia felt for her gown. A little mystery was supposed to be more arousing, wasn't it? And in case Marsh was inclined to put on his reading glasses and take a flashlight to search for stretch marks, she didn't have to make it easy for him. She had a few. Marsh had probably never even seen one before. Could she convince him that the tiny, silvery trails on the sides of her hips were scars from some dramatic life or death operation? What important organ could be reached through the hips?

She sighed again, finished chewing off her lipstick and fell asleep.

American

HEROES

AGAINST ALL ODDS

Just Deserts
Dixie
BROWNING

Silhouette Books

Published by Silhouette Books
America's Publisher of Contemporary Romance

For Pam Browning, who gave me the music,
and for Elaine Raco Chase, who gave me the line,
"Real men don't..." and for all the Persias

SILHOUETTE BOOKS
300 East 42nd St.,
New York, N. Y. 10017

ISBN 0-373-82238-3

JUST DESERTS

Copyright © 1984 by Dixie Browning

This edition published by arrangement with Harlequin Books S.A.

® and TM are trademarks of Harlequin Books S.A., used under license.
Trademarks indicated with ® are registered in the United States Patent
and Trademark Office, the Canadian Trade Marks Office and in other
countries.

Visit Silhouette at www.eHarlequin.com

Printed in U.S.A.

About the Author

Dixie Browning has been writing for Silhouette since 1980 and recently celebrated the publication of her sixty-fifth book, *Texas Millionaire*. She has also written a number of historical romances with her sister under the name Bronwyn Williams. An award-winning painter and writer, Browning lives on the Outer Banks of North Carolina. You may write to her at P.O. Box 1389, Buxton, NC 27920.

Books by Dixie Browning

Silhouette Desire

Shadow of Yesterday #68
Image of Love #91
The Hawk and the Honey #111
Late Rising Moon #121
Stormwatch #169
The Tender Barbarian #188
Matchmaker's Moon #212
A Bird in the Hand #234
In the Palm of Her Hand #264
A Winter Woman #324
There Once Was a Lover #337
Fate Takes a Holiday #403
Along Came Jones #427
Thin Ice #474
Beginner's Luck #517
Ships in the Night #541
Twice in a Blue Moon #588
Just Say Yes #637
Not a Marrying Man #678
Gus and the Nice Lady #691
Best Man for the Job #720
Hazards of the Heart #780
Kane's Way #801
*Keegan's Hunt #820
*Lucy and the Stone #853
*Two Hearts, Slightly Used #890
†Alex and the Angel #949
†The Beauty, the Beast and
   the Baby #985
The Baby Notion #1011
†Stryker's Wife #1033
Look What the Stork Brought #1111
‡The Passionate G-Man #1141
‡A Knight in Rusty Armor #1195
Texas Millionaire #1232
The Bride-in-Law #1251
§A Bride for Jackson Powers #1273

Silhouette Yours Truly

Single Female (Reluctantly) Seeks...

*Outer Banks
†Tall, Dark and Handsome
‡The Lawless Heirs
§The Passionate Powers

Silhouette Special Edition

Finders Keepers #50
Reach Out To Cherish #110
Just Deserts #181
Time and Tide #205
By Any Other Name #228
The Security Man #314
Belonging #414

Silhouette Romance

Unreasonable Summer #12
Tumbled Wall #38
Chance Tomorrow #53
Wren of Paradise #73
East of Today #93
Winter Blossom #113
Renegade Player #142
Island on the Hill #164
Logic of the Heart #172
Loving Rescue #191
A Secret Valentine #203
Practical Dreamer #221
Visible Heart #275
Journey to Quiet Waters #292
The Love Thing #305
First Things Last #323
Something for Herself #381
Reluctant Dreamer #460
A Matter of Timing #527
The Homing Instinct #747
Cinderella's Midnight Kiss #1450

Harlequin Historicals—
Writing as Bronwyn Williams

White Witch #3
Dandelion #23
Stormwalker #47
Gideon's Fall #67
The Mariner's Bride #99

Silhouette Books

Silhouette Christmas Stories 1987
"Henry the Ninth"

Spring Fancy 1994
"Grace and the Law"

World's Most Eligible Bachelors
‡His Business, Her Baby

Dear Reader,

I love this story! Forgive me if that sounds immodest, but reading it for the first time in more than sixteen years, it was like seeing old friends after years apart. Some things have changed since then...some things never change. The dreamy, steamy southern summertime, the delectable South Carolina recipes. Heroes and heroines in all their beautiful, infinite variety.

Want to know the real reason I wrote this book? Because I got sick and tired of reading about slender, fragile, exquisite blondes! And if you are one, then I'm sorry, but heroines come in more than one size. Persia's hero just happens to be wonderfully discerning, as well as terminally sexy. Not perfect—not quite, but then, who wants to live with a perfect man?

I love these people, their very human strengths and weaknesses, and their friends. Come on, join the house party—you'll feel right at home.

Dixie Browning

Please address questions and book requests to:
Silhouette Reader Service
U.S.: 3010 Walden Ave., P.O. Box 1325, Buffalo, NY 14269
Canadian: P.O. Box 609, Fort Erie, Ont. L2A 5X3

Chapter One

Persia scanned the graffiti on the rest room wall while she waited to wash her hands. "Pretty racy," she murmured to the woman in the pink polyester pantsuit who was touching up her lipstick in front of the mirror. "Must be the influence of the Speedway." The woman shot her a mystified look.

"Racing? Speedway?" Persia said helpfully. She shrugged as the woman capped her lipstick, dropped it into her bag, and hurriedly pushed her way through the swinging door. So much for a sense of humor. Whoever said laugh and the world laughs with you evidently hadn't tried cracking speedway jokes in Darlington, South Carolina.

Or maybe the woman simply had better taste in jokes. Persia's was notoriously bad, thanks to too many years of settling for "jolly" when she couldn't manage "thin."

Running cold water over her wrists in an effort to defeat the heat, she allowed her eyes to return to the mirror. Impulsively, she puffed out her cheeks and scowled. *Damn!* After all her good intentions, she'd blown it again. So maybe ten pounds had been a little unrealistic, but even five would have helped. With a loss of five pounds plus the strategic use of blusher, she'd have had cheekbones again.

As she recalled the admiring look on the face of the man who'd checked her oil and filled her tank, a whimsical smile replaced the scowl. Not every man wanted a bag of bones and a hank hair, she reassured herself. The smile faltered. Not every man did, but Marsh might.

The smile faded completely, leaving a spark of irritation in her large dark eyes. "Forget it, dreamer. Marsh is probably married by now," she reminded herself. In fact, he was probably fat and bald, and given to post-prandial naps. It had been ten years since she'd seen him—time enough for her to have outgrown this childish obsession with fairy tales. Or with one fairy tale, at least. And one Prince Charming in particular.

She gave herself a last critical look before going back outside into the late May heat. She should have known better than to try and make the trip in one day. The makeup she'd applied so carefully before daylight this morning had melted, and the cornflower-blue dress she'd had so many compliments on was limp and rumpled. At least her cheeks didn't have to rely on blusher for their color, nor her lashes on mascara for length and lustrousness.

She paid for her gas, tucked a wayward strand of dark hair back in place, and slid into her ovenlike car. Darn it, she'd had almost three weeks to get in shape for this house party, three weeks to become so lean and glamorous that one look at her and Marsh would instantly forget all about the last time he'd seen her.

As soon as she'd read Tom and Kathy's invitation to come and bring her fiancé to a tenth anniversary reunion of their wedding party, her mind had feverishly gone to work on the scenario. Now, as she neared her destination, she pictured the coming reunion. They'd all be there—people she hadn't seen in years. Tom and Kathy Gaillard, of course, and Tom's best man, William Marshall Randolph the third.

Persia always had trouble dragging her mind past that particular name. She made one last attempt to quell her stage fright at the coming reunion and put things into perspective. Marilee Dunn would be there of course, probably with that Midas type she'd married. Marilee and Kathy had been good friends all through high school, although Persia could never quite understand why. They were totally different.

Who else? There'd been several ushers, but the only one she could recall was Tom's younger brother, Chip, who at seventeen had been a master of the veiled insult. He'd since married one of Persia's old classmates. For the sake of all concerned, Persia hoped he'd outgrown that streak of quiet maliciousness that had once made her life hell.

Persia squinted against the late afternoon sun and cast back in her memory to one of the more miserable periods of her life; her cousin Kathy's wedding. Judy Alice Fishburn and poor Susan Cowan had been attendants, too, but it had been Marilee who'd stage-managed the whole affair. Marilee had been the one who'd chosen those atrocious pink, ruffled gowns. And of course, Marilee, red hair and all, had looked stunning in hers. In all honesty Persia didn't think it had been deliberate, but if she'd tried, she couldn't have come up with a style less flattering to someone who was called Baby Blimp by her classmates.

Well, this time Persia was doing the choosing. If this tenth anniversary house party spelled the end of a long-held fantasy for her, at least she'd carry it off in style. She'd shot her clothing budget for the next five years, and it was going to be worth every penny of it. This time, no one was going to feel sorry for poor pink, plump Persia.

Even minus a fiancé. She'd told Kathy simply that Patrick couldn't make it. She'd have to find time to explain that the engagement was off before Kathy started lining up a wedding present, but there was no point in elaborating. The fact that she'd been unceremoniously dumped only six weeks earlier wasn't the sort of news one bruited about at an anniversary party.

Persia waited for the twinge of emotion that usually came when she thought about Patrick and his mother. It didn't come. She shrugged and considered the fact that deep down, she must be extremely shallow. Scarcely a month had gone by and already she'd breezed past heartbreak and was back at her old pastime.

Daydreaming. Fantasizing—just because she was going to be seeing Marsh again after all this time. She really should be ashamed of herself for being more concerned with an ancient infatuation than with a newly broken engagement. On the other hand, it was good to know what a resiliant organ the heart really was. Two weeks was a long time to expose herself to someone as devastating as Marsh Randolph.

It had been rough, but she'd finished up a day early and driven straight through just to get to Pinopolis a day ahead of the others. By the time Marsh arrived, she'd be all ready. She'd deliberately planned it so that she'd have plenty of time to put on her lean, languid lady look. For that, she'd decided on the black linen sundress, with a black leghorn picture hat drooping casually from her fingers, and a pair of designer sunglasses that ended just above what was supposed to have been the hollows of her cheeks.

"Darlings," she'd drawl in her best lean, langorous manner. "How *lovely* to see you all!"

Oh, yes, she'd rehearsed the scene in her mind a hundred times. She'd be on the veranda with Kathy and Tom when Marsh drove up. Her cousin Kathy, as bubbly as her dark-haired husband was droll, would dash out to meet the car, and Tom, meerschaum in hand, would saunter out behind her. He'd take Marsh's bag, and the two men would slap each other on the shoulder and exchange lies about how they hadn't changed a bit, and then...

Here the picture always blurred. "Marsh," Persia would exclaim huskily from her graceful pose on the glider. "How lovely to see you again. I'm Persia Abernathy, one of the bridesmaids." She didn't especially want him digging back into his memory to try and place her; the less he recalled of that first meeting, the better.

And if he wasn't alone? What then? "This must be your wife," she'd say sweetly. "I'm delighted to meet you, Mrs. Randolph. And these are the children?"

What could she say about Marsh's children, except that she'd give her wisdom teeth and any other spare parts to have been their mother? And wouldn't *that* send a few eyebrows sky high? Poor Kathy, who'd never had an indiscreet thought in her life, would be in shock.

No, Persia promised herself—she wouldn't embarrass the Gaillards and their house party by dredging up that ancient adolescent passion. Besides, she'd promised herself to exorcise all that old agony once and for all.

At sixteen she'd been jealous of her cousin, and horribly guilty about it. Kathy was petite, blue-eyed, and blond—everything Persia was not—and the whole world adored her. She'd been marrying her childhood sweetheart, and from a multitude of friends, she'd chosen as one of her attendants her cousin Persia Abernathy—barely sixteen, five feet eight, forty pounds overweight, and excruciatingly shy. Kathy, whose parents had "family," but little money, had used the size of the tiny church as an excuse to limit the size of the wedding, and Persia had felt inordinately proud of being a part of it all.

Proud, that is, until she'd tried on the gown Marilee had picked for the attendants. It was bright camellia pink, approximately the shade of Persia's complexion at the time, and the bouffant skirt was a nightmare of organdy Scarlett O'Hara ruffles.

Persia had seriously considered joining the woman's auxiliary of the Foreign Legion, but she hadn't her own passport, and besides, she'd used up her monthly allowance on Beatle albums and chocolate-covered cherries.

Ignoring the disastrous sunburn Persia had collected the day before the wedding, Kathy had assured her that the color was marvelous with her dark hair and her truly beautiful eyes. Numb with misery, Persia had gone through the motions with all the grace and enthusiasm of a pink ruffled beanbag. Nor had it helped that she'd just met Tom's best man, Marsh Randolph, and been stricken by an intensely painful case of love at first sight.

Opening the car window to breathe in the essence of honeysuckle and sun-warmed earth, she surrendered herself to the low country humidity. It had been years since she'd been back, but it was still the same. Backlighted by a late afternoon sun, the irrigated fields glowed with color against the hazy darkness of the woods. Blue-green wheat, silver-green oats, and acres of peach trees, heavy with unripe fruit. Like a sentinel of another era, an occasional dead pine tree rose high above the surrounding woods, it's barkless arms silvery with age.

As a landscape architect, Persia was familiar with the signs of poor soil; even so, it was the fallow fields, ablaze with fiery sheep sorrel or blanketed with shimmering lavender wildflowers, that brought an ache to her throat. She'd always loved this region, with its tall, somber pines, its moss-hung oaks, its bald cypresses. She'd missed it far more than she'd realized. Virginia, where she now lived, was still the South, but it was a different sort of South. The impeccably kept farms and estates around Spotsylvania County had little in common with this part of South Carolina.

"Come back to earth, Persia," she muttered, braking after she'd zoomed past the reduce-speed sign near Eutawville. How many times had her father said that to her? "Daydreams are a waste of time," she'd been warned over and over again.

Her father had been right, of course. Unfortunately, Persia had inherited the wrong genes from the family pool. She'd definitely been shortchanged on common sense. As for the rest of her senses, those were abundantly developed—as witness her constant battle to resist food when she knew darned well that her metabolism couldn't handle it properly. As witness her weakness for perfumes, for rich fabrics and blatantly romantic music.

As witness her adolescent fantasy that one day she'd see Marsh again and he'd fall at her feet, smitten with the sultry beauty of her chocolate-colored eyes and her coffee-colored hair—not to mention her occasional cheekbones and the waistline she worked so diligently to maintain.

Oh, it was a relatively harmless fantasy. As fantasies went, this one even had its practical applications. More than once she'd used the dream of meeting him again as a carrot to lure her into launching herself on another diet. Then, after three days of starvation, she'd rationalize her inevitable lapse by telling herself that she'd never see him again, and if she did, he'd never recognize her—and if he did, he certainly wasn't going to be bowled off his pins by the mere sight of her curvaceous new figure. So what difference did one more fudge brownie made in the cosmic scheme of things?

On a more realistic level, she'd do better to hope he

didn't remember. Just because she'd shaped up enough to collect a few compliments—and even a heart or two—since then, didn't mean that she'd succeeded in evicting that pudgy, miserably self-conscious sixteen-year-old. Underneath the budget-busting wardrobe she'd chosen for this wingding, there still lurked a trace of the pathetic creature who'd fallen so madly in love with a hopelessly inaccessible man that ten years later she could still recall the scent of his cologne.

As she neared the turnoff to Pinopolis, her throat grew dry and her palms grew moist. This had to stop! She simply *had* to get rid of all these childish, nonproductive fantasies before she met him again, or she'd end up making an idiot of herself in front of the whole house party. Good Lord, she'd only known him for three days—two and a half, to be precise. If she started palpitating every time she got within ten feet of him, it was going to prove embarrassing to all concerned.

Persia looked around her eagerly as Kathy led her up to the rambling old house Tom's grandparents had bought shortly after the power company had dammed up the rivers to form the Santee-Cooper Lakes complex. Pinopolis had been the highest ground in the area, once highly favored by the residents of the lower, malaria-plagued Charleston. There were several stately old homes on the tiny peninsula that was all that remained of the high ground. Many more were at the bottom of Lake Moultrie. "It's changed—and yet it hasn't."

"Pinopolis or the house?" Tom asked, taking Persia's bags from her hands.

"Both. I noticed several new houses—nice ones, too. Bloody swank. Who's idea was it to paint this place gray?"

"Kathy's."

"Tom's."

"Fighting already, hmmm?" Persia teased. "I knew it wouldn't last. Who's here?" She followed the couple inside, noting with pleasure that although the sprawling, seventy-year-old house had been refurbished, it was still much the same inside as when Persia and Kathy had visited the Gaillards there as children.

"Chip'll be here most anytime—if he doesn't forget altogether. The others will be here tomorrow."

"I was so surprised to hear he married Ann Vairey—she's a doll. I'm looking forward to seeing her again."

Tom placed the two suitcases inside a second-floor bedroom that was tucked cozily up under the eaves. Kathy's eyes clouded and slid away as she said, "Ann won't be coming. She and Chip have separated."

"Oh, no. I'm so sorry." Persia meant it. She'd always liked Ann, even though she'd wondered at her taste in marrying Chip Gaillard. Chip was generally conceded to be a genius, but that didn't make him any easier to take. He'd teased Persia unmercifully back when the Gaillards and the Abernathys had lived in one another's pockets. Persia's family had lived in the Forest Drive area of Columbia. Kathy's family had lived a few blocks away in a much smaller house, but the two Abernathy families and the Gaillards had been close friends for generations.

Over dinner, Persia caught up on the news. She'd lost contact when she'd stayed on in Fredericksburg after graduating from Mary Washington College in Virginia. Her own immediate family was gone, her mother having died when Persia was thirteen, and her father four years ago.

"Tom's opening an office in Charleston the first of August," Kathy told her proudly.

"Great," Persia commented, reaching for another hush puppy and then reconsidering. She'd had only one fried catfish—the smallest one on the platter. And no french fries. "What about the others? I haven't kept up with any of them since I left home to go to school." *What about Marsh?* she meant. *Where is he? What's he doing? Has he married?* Kathy had mentioned once in a rare phone call that his father had remarried and moved to France, but Persia had been far too tongue-tied to ask about Marsh.

Kathy excused herself to bring in the peach cobbler, and Persia groaned.

"Let's see—Billy Palmer's in West Germany with IBM. The Kelsey boys are both white-water guides somewhere out in California. Who else? You knew about poor Susan's broken legs, I guess," Kathy murmured, dishing up generous servings of the luscious-looking dessert and adding a big dollop of whipped cream. "I wrote you about that, didn't I? She always was a daredevil, but skydiving? I never even got up nerve enough to go off the high board at the club."

"None for me, Kath, thanks."

Kathy's wide blue eyes took on a wounded look as they went from her beautiful dessert to her cousin's nicely proportioned, if still generous, figure. "Oh, come on, just a little bit won't hurt you. I'll leave off the whipped cream, all right?"

"No, honestly, I couldn't, Kath. I've been munching all the way from Fredericksburg," Persia lied.

"Well, I think you're being mean, but—tell you what. I'll just put yours in the refrigerator, and you can have it before you go to bed."

"Sure." Persia sighed, hoping against hope that she wouldn't give in to either frustration or temptation. "What about Judy Alice?"

"Pregnant again. She's due any day now, so she won't be coming. She married that Cross boy, remember? They've got three of the darlin'est little boys."

"So that leaves…?" Persia prompted, pleating her napkin nervously in her lap. If Marsh wasn't coming, she was going to curl up and die. Or eat every last bite of Kathy's peach cobbler—which wouldn't solve anything.

"Marsh is coming. He's going to be here the whole two weeks, and he'll be bringing Marilee, of course. She's back in Columbia now, since the divorce."

"The divorce?" Persia echoed sinkingly.

"That old thing she married—the one who owns that hotel in Chicago? She left him, didn't you hear? Honestly, nobody knew why she married him in the first place—she was practically engaged to Marsh. So far, I haven't been able to find out what happened. That old man actually sent her to some sort of a seminar about investments, can you imagine? The few times I've seen her since she left him, that's all she wants to talk about. Honestly, Persia, if we weren't practically like sisters, I'd be bored stiff."

She scraped the last of the whipped cream from her dish. "Still, maybe it paid off. The first thing she did when she came back home was to buy herself a house just down the street from the old Ravenel mansion. I wonder what Marsh thinks. He still lives in the same old apartment he took when his father remarried."

Persia's heart fell with an almost audible thud. "So I guess Marsh isn't married yet." As if it mattered now. Marilee obviously already had him in the bag, and Persia—even the new and improved version—was no match for someone like Marilee Dunn.

Damn it, she was always out of phase! Once she'd been on the same financial and social level with the Dunns and the Randolphs, but they'd been grownup and she'd been sixteen—and not a Brooke Shields sort of sixteen, either, but a real mess.

And then, shortly before her father had died, he'd gambled everything on a long shot and lost. After that, Persia's lifestyle had undergone a drastic change. She'd been thoroughly shaken, not only by the loss of her father, but also by the forced sale of the only home she'd ever known. When the estate had been settled, there'd been only a few thousand dollars left.

In an impulsive move she'd never once regretted, she'd put the whole amount down on a half acre and a tiny frame house several miles south of Fredericksburg. Her job paid reasonably well, and as the economy improved, there was every reason to believe she'd do even better. At twenty-six she was a home owner. How many women could make that statement?

But let's face it; people like Marsh and Marilee *hired* gardeners—they didn't socialize with them. And degree or no degree, fancy title or not, Persia was a gardener, who liked nothing better than to get her bare hands into rich, fertile loam.

Later that night, as she lay awake in her uncomfortable heirloom bed under the sloping eaves, Persia tried to quell the excitement that simmered just under the surface of her mind. Tomorrow she'd know the truth. Time and her imagination had probably created a golden Greek god out of a depressingly ordinary man. For the sake of her peace of mind, she hoped so. To be completely objective, his nose *was* slightly too large, and his smile *did* turn down at the corners—and his hair was so thick it was almost impossible to groom properly. And since the day she'd drenched him with pink champagne punch and then almost knocked him off his feet, she'd been haunted by the memory of those sage-green eyes, that caramel-colored hair, and that velvety drawl of his.

Would he recognize her? Not even in her most elaborate fantasies did she imagine that he'd been poring over those wedding pictures the way she had. She'd carried them all through the four years at Mary Washington and then later on, while she'd been busy working days and going to school nights to earn herself a more marketable degree in horticulture. She suspected that he'd been a sort of subliminal yardstick against which she'd measured all men. Pat had almost measured up—almost, but not quite.

A thread of tension uncoiled somewhere in the pit of her stomach and spread its warmth into her thighs. What would that hair feel like under her fingers? What would that wide, firm mouth taste like—how would it feel on her own mouth, on her...

Damn it, this had to stop, or she'd never get any sleep! Yesterday she'd personally delivered fourteen twelve-foot willow oaks and supervised the planting herself, and then gotten up before daylight and driven flat out to get here. And now, thanks to an overactive imagination and an underworked libido, she was going to be counting sheep all night long. Oh, she'd look terrific tomorrow! She really would!

Marsh angled the vent away from him. He despised air conditioning and used it only as a last resort, but the wind blew Marilee's hair, and he'd rolled up his window and switched it on as soon as they'd left town. His reward had been a smile that promised more than it usually delivered.

His mind on business matters, he murmured an occasional automatic response as Marilee detailed the troubles she'd had locating just the right shade of green for the gameroom carpet.

"Hmmm," he commented absently.

"It will increase the value of...Marsh, you haven't heard a word I've said since we left home. If you're going to be this way the whole time we're at the Gaillards', then I'd just as soon not bother."

"Sorry, honey." He cast her a swift, apologetic smile and returned his attention to his driving. "The meeting last night lasted until I couldn't see straight, and then I had a couple of appointments first things this morning.''

"You'll never learn to delegate, will you? Freddie always says—''

He could do without Fred Kurtz. The name had stuck in his craw since the first time he'd ever heard it. "Newspapers and hotels are two different things, Marilee.'' Deliberately, he relaxed his grip on the wheel. "It'll be good to unwind for a couple of weeks. I've been needing an excuse.''

"I'm not sure how relaxing it will be, with a house full of people, but if it gets too rowdy we can always go on down to Charleston, just the two of us. There's a man there I've been wanting you to meet—he's putting together a limited partnership—real estate. If we get a chance, let's slip away for a few days, shall we? Besides, we've both been so rushed lately that we haven't even had time to talk about—personal matters.''

"Hmmm. Yeah—I'm looking forward to a real vacation for a change. No pressures, no shop talk. We used to have a lot of fun with Tom and Kathy, remember?''

Marilee Kurtz, née Dunn, touched the sprayed perfection of her copper-colored hair and sighed. "As much as I adore Kathy, we really don't have all that much in common anymore. She's into playing the perfect little housewife, and Lord knows I'd die before I'd settle for anything so deadly dull. Freddie would have laughed himself silly if I'd put on a ruffled apron and headed for the kitchen.''

Flashing her an amused glance, Marsh teased her. "Did you even have a kitchen?''

"I heard there was one up there somewhere, but I never actually saw it. Otto, the hotel's chef, was one of Switzerland's national treasures until Freddie lured him over here after The Parker Lakefront stole François from us.''

"The old Gaillard summer place might be a far cry from

your penthouse on North Michigan, but I'd match Kathy's cooking against your Otto's anyday.''

"Sure, if you like everything fried or smothered in cream. Oh, Marsh, don't mind me. I know how much you've been looking forward to this trip. It's going to be marvelous—really, darling. I haven't had a minute to visit with Kathy in ages, and we were always so close.'' She sighed. "But let's face it—the only thing we have in common these days is the fact that we were classmates in high school, and we wouldn't even have that if Daddy hadn't been on one of his democratic kicks and refused to let me go to private school.''

Marsh drove in silence for several miles. A drift of Marilee's perfume reached his nostrils and he inhaled appreciatively. It was a scent he'd given her for her birthday. He hadn't been sure she'd really liked it—for a moment, he'd imagined he saw a quick look of disappointment.

She broke into the silence, her carefully modulated voice expressing doubt. "I only hope the whole wedding party doesn't show up for this thing. Can you imagine that old lake house of theirs packed to the sills with the likes of Billy Palmer and all those cotton-haired children of Judy Alice's?''

Marsh shrugged. "I've borne up under worse fates. By the way, I ran into Judy and her boys downtown not long ago. Looks like she and Cappy might be trying for a girl.''

"Oh, Lord, some people breed like flies.''

Marsh's lips turned down at the corners as he turned off Highway 6 for the short drive out onto the peninsula that was Pinopolis. Beside him, Marilee made last-minute repairs to her flawlessly groomed hair and then brushed an imaginary speck from her pink silk skirt. On the hottest day of August, Marsh mused, she'd look just as cool as she did now. The woman was amazing.

* * *

"Persia, see if you can reach that jar up on the top shelf." Kathy had checked out her staples, found them lacking, and sent Tom into Moncks Corner with a long list. "I can never remember from month to month what I've left here and what I need to bring."

Persia handed down the empty blue jar. She was still flushed from sunbathing—at least she told herself that the sun was responsible for the glow on her face. Could sunburn bring a glow to one's eyes, as well?

"If you don't need me for anything, I think I'll go get a shower and change into something frankly ravishing. Just the thought of Marilee is enough to give me an inferiority complex."

"Oh, hon, you look wonderful! Honestly, you always did have a beautiful face, and on you a few extra pounds look good—and there aren't really all that many extra ones."

"For the large, economy size, maybe," Persia allowed. "I'm doing my darndest to get down one more size, but you don't help much with your fried fish and peach cobbler." Persia laughed as she started upstairs. She'd managed to save herself from the cobbler last night, only to be defeated by Kathy's breakfast of ham biscuits and buttered hominy grits.

A few minutes later she shut off the shower and reached for a Hawaiian print muumuu. Her dryer was out of sorts, and her hair was both long and thick, but half an hour out on the pier in the sun and breeze would do the job.

Sliding her feet into flowered scuffs, she annointed her face with a mild sunscreen and hurried downstairs. In spite of her dark coloring, she burned easily until she had a good basecoat of tan. It was coming along nicely, thanks to spending almost as much time on the site as she did at the drawing board, but remembering the last time she'd seen Marsh, she didn't dare take chances.

"Be back in half an hour to help get lunch," she sang out as she skipped the two last steps and dashed out the front door. The mid-morning sun struck her blindingly as she emerged from the deep shade of the veranda, and before she could put on the brakes she slammed into a tall, luggage-laden figure.

"Good Lord—!"

"Oh, gosh, I'm so sorry!" Persia cried, pushing up the damp towel full of hair that had fallen over her face. "I didn't see…you," she finished weakly, gazing up with a sense of déjà vu into an achingly familiar face.

"No problem," Marsh said easily. "I'm Marsh Randolph, and this is Marilee Kurtz. I don't seem to recall…"

"Persia?" Marilee said wonderingly. "Can it really be you? Darling, what have you done to yourself? You look positively *gaunt!* Doesn't she look gaunt, Marsh? You remember little Persia Abernathy, Kathy's cousin. My goodness, you've changed so much I hardly knew you. You must have lost tons!"

Embarrassment swept over her in agonizing waves as she stood there, helpless to extricate herself. In spite of the fact that she towered over the smaller woman and outweighed her by an indecent number of pounds, she felt small. She felt *tiny.* She felt like a loathesome insect about to be crushed under an elegant, size-four shoe.

"Marsh! Marilee—come in, come in!" Kathy slammed out the screened door and bounced down the steps. "I didn't even hear you drive up! Tom's gone to the grocery store, but he'll—oh, and you remember Persia, don't you? Come on in!" the petite blonde cried out, taking each of them by the arm. "Where have y'all been keeping yourselves lately?"

Sitting cross-legged on the end of the pier moments later, Persia toweled the ends of her hair ruthlessly. She might as well give up! After all her plans, he had to catch her wearing this damned flowered circus tent! The black linen had been a rotten idea, anyway, she decided morosely. Nobody dressed up around here.

But it looked so good on her. It made her complexion look like beige satin, and her eyes look enormous, and the style did marvelous things for her figure. The minute she'd seen it, something in her mind had gone *click!* It had cost the earth, and she'd rushed in and bought it before she'd had time to come to her senses. It was the magic dress that was going to make all her dreams come true. Just like the diet books that lined her shelf. Each time she gained a few more pounds, she'd race out and buy another diet book, as if the act itself would do the trick.

That cursed imagination of hers! It was one thing to be able to look at a set of blueprints and visualize a whole landscaping concept. It was another thing altogether to look at a dress in a shop window and weave a complete love story around it.

She stayed out as long as she dared, and then she stood up and scowled at the hospitable old house under the pines, with its high brick foundation, its red painted tin roof, its gray clapboards and wide, shady porches. She could feel perspiration prickling her skin under the cumbersome polished cotton. Its flowing lines and colorful design had looked terrific on the mannequin, but evidently it lost something in the translation.

Sucking in her cheeks, she plodded toward the house. By contrast, at least, her face might look thin, Gaunt, as Marilee had called it. Damn it, how could that woman be even more beautiful than she had been ten years ago? With hair like polished copper and eyes the color of Thompson's Seedless grapes, she'd always been stunning, but there was a new sureness about her now—a subtle something that made Persia want to crawl into a hole somewhere and lick her wounds.

Tom drove up just as she reached the house. Plastering a parody of a smile on her face, she angled across the pinestraw-covered lawn to meet him. "Marsh and Marilee are here," she announced brightly.

"I thought that was his car. I guess when Chip gets here, that will complete the list. Shame the rest couldn't make it, but I guess it was pretty short notice." He handed over a paper sack and leaned inside to extract another one. "Too heavy for you? We just got this idea when I knew we'd be moving to Charleston, and it seemed like a good way to get together with old friends. Kathy told you we've got tickets to the G&R Club dance on Saturday, didn't she?"

"I brought along a dress," Persia said dully. While Tom carried in a crate of soft drinks, Persia took the two sacks of groceries into the kitchen and put them away. Kathy was in the living room with Marsh and Marilee, catching up on the news. By the time the last item was put away in the kitchen, Tom had joined them for drinks.

It was worse than she'd even imagined. He looked stunning! That same crinkly grin still warmed his rather tough features. She stuck her head in the door. "Everything's put away. I'm going up to change, so if you need me, just yell." As she passed the luggage still stacked at the head of the stairs, it occurred to her to wonder if Marsh and Marilee would be sharing. Ten years ago Marilee wouldn't have considered it—at least, not under these circumstances, but times change, and there was really no reason why they shouldn't share a room if they were sleeping together and everyone knew it.

And if they did, she didn't think she could stand it! Raking a brush through her long, dark brown hair, Persia fought against sinking back into the no-win situation of an imaginary, one-sided love affair. She'd come here to work Marsh Randolph out of her system once and for all, she reminded herself sternly. It should be just that much easier since he was obviously involved with someone else. So why wasn't she jumping for joy?

Because she wasn't. One look at those sage-green eyes of his, that crooked, downturned smile, and she was in worse shape than she had been ten years ago when she'd landed him a flying tackle and drenched his wedding clothes with champagne punch. She'd watched him at the reception as he danced first with the bride, then with the maid of honor, and then with Judy and Susan. Looking like the epitome of every woman's dream in his wedding finery, he'd handed Susan over to her fiancé and then turned to survey the crowd.

Persia had been achingly aware of every move he'd made. She'd seen his eyes pass over her and then flash back, and then he'd excused himself and begun to make his way through the crowd. A bundle of pure, raw agony, she'd stopped breathing the moment his eyes had flicked her. By the time he reached her, she was almost cataleptic, her gaze glued to the toe of her pink silk pumps. Squeezing the damp stem of her glass, she'd fought against a wave of panic. And then, like watching a slow motion film, she watched his hand reach out to her—square, tanned, its back lightly furred in gold. Only his hand—not to mention his eyes—went right past her, and she heard Marilee's sugar coated drawl saying, "Marsh, it's about time you got through with all your duty dances. Take me out to the garden, darling, I can't stand being crushed up in the middle of all these hot bodies."

Mortified—she was nothing if not a hot body—Persia had stepped back hastily and tripped on a dragging ruffle. In an effort to right herself, she'd stepped forward. The camellia pink punch—Marilee's touch, again—had gone all over Marsh's pristine white front, and Persia had stumbled against him, driving him into the back of the minister's mother, who had muttered something surprisingly colorful.

Marsh had recovered quickly, apologized to the dowager, and then, with a smile so kind it had paralyzed her, he'd dragged Persia to the ladies lounge, where he'd instructed the attendant to look after her.

He'd disappeared then. She hadn't seen him again, but later she'd heard that he'd turned up at the tail end of the festivities in jeans and a blazer, and that he and Marilee had spent the weekend together at Myrtle Beach.

Chapter Two

She couldn't avoid them forever. Reluctantly, Persia took a last look at herself in the mirror. Was it her imagination, or did these turquoise pants make her hips look wider? She'd paid a king's ransom for the two-piece silk outfit after the sales clerk had said turquoise did magical things for her coloring.

Actually, the color was rather good on her. Her heavy-cream complexion was turning a nice shade of honey-tan, thank goodness. At least she wouldn't be a walking reminder of the time when, two days before the wedding, she'd decided to get the full season's dose in one day. She'd had some foolish idea that if dark shades were more slenderizing than pale ones, she'd lose fifteen pounds in one day—optically.

It had been disastrous. Her father had been furious with her, and Lucy, the housekeeper, had soaked her in baking soda, doused her in vinegar, and then gone out and bought a large-sized box of medium face powder.

She stuck her head in the door of the living room. "Do I need to do anything for lunch?" she asked hopefully. She'd stayed upstairs for almost an hour, and she still couldn't summon enough poise to go in and join Marsh and Marilee.

"No problem. The salads are ready except for dressing, I've made black bean soup, and the corn sticks are in the oven."

Persia stiffled her groan. Marsh in one room, food in the other. This was going to be tougher than she'd imagined. Trust Kathy to drag out all her old favorite recipes. One of the abiding family jokes had been that on their wedding day, the brothers Madison and Gregory Abernathy had presented their respective brides with a copy of the family cookbook.

Marilee was still wearing the pink silk shirtwaister she'd arrived in, but Marsh had changed into a navy knit shirt and a pair of snug white rugby pants.

Give me strength, Persia prayed silently as she took a chair on the far side of the room from the men. It wasn't fair for any man to have such narrow hips—especially when they were crouched over a tackle box, with the demarcation line between tanned and untanned flesh clearly visible.

While Tom and Marsh discussed the comparative merits of various lures, Persia smiled grimly and dealt with Marilee's questions about how much she had lost and how far she still had to go.

"Well, actually," she murmured, wondering if Marilee had any idea how offensive her questions were, "I'll always have a battle on my hands. I'm one of those people who can gain five pounds just by reading a cookbook." She glanced at the corner where the men were so engrossed. This wasn't her idea of scintillating small talk, but if Marilee got a thrill out of learning how the other half live, she'd oblige her. Up to a point.

Marilee's classical features took on a vaguely hallowed expression. "It's a simple matter of calories, Persia. Just use your willpower and cut down just a *wee* bit on everything, you'll be all right. Believe me, I know what I'm talking about—I ballooned up to a size ten right after Freddie and I were married. Honestly, I looked awful! I was too embarrassed to set foot out of the hotel until I'd starved myself back down to a normal size again."

Persia wondered what it would feel like to wrap her hands around a clump of that orange hair and pull. "I'm sure it must have been dreadful," she oozed sympathetically. "I was *born* wearing a size ten."

"Come and get it," Kathy sang out from the kitchen that jutted off from the back of the house.

Marilee winced. Marsh straightened up, caught sight of Persia, and grinned. "My favorite song—how about you?"

He'd been eavesdropping! How could he be so cruel? Wasn't it enough that she had to put up with Marilee's well-meaning tactlessness?

Oh, great Scott, she was being paranoid. It had been merely a friendly remark, and if she was going to start searching for hidden meanings in every word anyone uttered, she may as well pack her bags and leave. She'd gone through years of that sort of agony, and not for any foolish fantasy was she going to repeat it.

Taking her place at the round oak table, she struggled to overcome her unexpected attack of gaucherie. Funny— she'd never been particularly sensitive around Patrick, or any of the other men she'd dated over the past several years. Of course, they'd never known her at her heaviest. She'd trimmed down considerably during her freshman year at Mary Washington, to the point where she actually had "measurements." So they happened to be several inches more, respectively, than her friends' measurements—at least it was obvious where her hips left off and her waist began.

She'd fought a good battle from then on, and gradually, as she'd trimmed down, her attitude about herself had changed. It hadn't been easy; she'd had to face the fact that she'd never be small. And after being teased unmercifully in her younger years and ignored all through high school—when she wasn't the butt of jokes—it had taken a bit of doing to convince herself that she was just as worthwhile a person as any of her thinner acquaintances. If she'd had an outstanding talent, it might have been easier to bear, but not one of her peers had considered a green thumb a viable accomplishment.

Part of the problem had been her own defensiveness— she'd looked for slights even where none had been intended, but gradually that had changed. It was only now, around people who'd known her *when,* that she found herself searching each word for hidden barbs. It was as if all those pounds she'd lost had come back to haunt her, like an oversized aura.

She played with the soup. It was delicious, as she well remembered, but in spite of the innocent lemon-bow garnish, it was seasoned with ham hock and loaded with butter and sherry. The corn sticks were totally irresistable, though, and she munched one of those as she gazed longingly at the egg-and-bacon-garnished wilted salad, its bib lettuce and spring onions glistening with a dressing of hot bacon drippings, vinegar, pepper and sugar. From now on she'd help with every meal, if only to look after her own interests.

"Aren't you eating your soup, Persia?" Kathy inquired. "It's Grandma Tat's recipe."

"We just had breakfast a little while ago," Persia protested.

"How's fishing?" Marsh asked, shaking his head when Kathy tried to press another serving of soup on him.

As plates were emptied, the talk turned to less personal matters. Persia headed for the kitchen to start the monumental cleanup. Kathy carried on the Abernathy tradition when it came to cooking, all right, but only at the expense of every utensil in the kitchen. Turning quickly away from the remains of the macaroon soufflé, she started running water into the sink.

By the time she'd finished and returned to the living room, there was no one in evidence except for Marsh and Marilee. "Where's everyone else?"

"Would you believe fishing?" Marilee sniffed. "Honestly, as if it weren't enough that poor Kathy slaves away in the kitchen all morning, she has to waste her afternoon baiting Tom's hooks. Instead of dragging her off fishing, he ought to be out hiring her a maid."

Persia took a wicker rocker on the far side of the room from Marsh. Extending her long curved legs, she leaned back against the faded chintz cushion. "Next to cooking, Kathy enjoys fishing better than anything. Don't you remember? Weekends when she wasn't too busy being Homecoming Queen or Prom Queen, she was always down here drowning worms. She knows every honey hole in Lake Moultrie."

"Ugh! Persia, do you have to be so graphic?" Marilee crossed her slender legs, and Persia drew hers up defensively.

Real men don't like taut thighs, she paraphrased in silent desperation, but it was no good. No matter how much she tried to comfort herself with pat phrases like, "You can't get too much of a good thing," the plain fact was that she was five inches taller and a good deal heavier than Marilee. And no matter how nicely those pounds were arranged on her large frame, no matter how proudly she carried herself, a small inner voice kept reminding her that according to today's standards of beauty, she was a second-class citizen.

The desultory conversation gradually evolved into a monologue as Marilee described the house in Columbia in which she'd invested part of her divorce settlement, and the penthouse in her ex-husband's hotel where they'd lived during their few years of marriage. It occurred to Persia that there was something almost indecent in gloating over the assets of a man one had just divorced. But then, to some people—and obviously Marilee was one of them— it was all a game. Divorce lawyers at fifty paces, and may the best man win.

Marsh appeared to be dozing. A shaft of midafternoon sun angled down across a rag rug, striking his knees and the toes of his deck shoes. Persia found her own lids growing heavy as the drone of Marilee's voice blended with the distant hum of an outboard motor and the buzz of the bees in the pittosporum outside the front window. Just before she went under for the third time, it occurred to her that she was sleeping with Marsh—and right before Marilee's eyes. She chuckled.

"What's wrong? Did I say something funny?" the redhead demanded petulantly.

"It's nothing," Persia muttered.

"How about a cold beer and a walk along the shore?" Marsh suggested, standing and stretching his arms over his head. His shirt slipped its moorings, and Persia's eyes were riveted to the pattern of hair that trailed down his flat stomach. It was surprisingly dark, considering that the hair on his head was the color of ripe wheat.

"You'll have to wait until I change," Marilee replied, rising with a gracefulness that had to have been bred in the bone. Her smile ignored Persia altogether. "I hope the mosquitoes aren't bad."

"Leave off the perfume, and you'll be okay," Marsh said easily.

"But darling, it's the one you gave me. If I have to choose between you and the mosquitoes..." She sighed, lifting her shoulders delicately as she pouted up at him. "I guess you win, hands down."

"Ye gads, such self-sacrifice," Persia muttered under her breath. She stood abruptly and strode across to the door. "I need some fresh air."

By the time she emerged into the heated brilliance of the cloudless afternoon, she was already regretting her small display of pettiness. Marilee was...Marilee. A hothouse blossom. She didn't pretend to be anything else. Was that any reason to despise her? Given the chance, Persia knew she'd change places with her in a minute.

No, she wouldn't. She was perfectly content with who she was, except in the matter of her size—and even that was under control. More or less. For the moment.

Grinning at her own mental qualifications, Persia headed for the narrow, shelving bank and skirted a cluster of cypress knees. She'd heard more than one short woman profess to envy her height, and even a few who complained of not being able to gain weight, but let's face it—thin was in, and short was petite, and ninety percent of the decent clothes available were for size twelve and under. Persia's build might be great for a Wagnerian diva, but who wanted to wear stainless steel bras and horned helmets all year round? It was just that she got so tired of seeing acres and acres of petite and junior sizes, and then being steered into a cramped corner where everything in her size range was squashed up on one short rack, as if size were contagious.

In the house Marsh, spinning rod in hand, hid his impatience and managed a dry smile as he heard Marilee's footsteps on the stairs. *How the hell could anyone spend forty-five minutes just changing a dress and a pair of shoes?* he wondered.

"Ready, darling? Oh, dear. You're not planning to take that thing along, are you? I thought you were just going to stroll around, maybe see who's built here since the last time I was here."

With only the briefest of hesitations, Marsh laid his new spinning rod in a rack with several of Tom's spares. Funny how he kept forgetting little things about Marilee—but then, they'd been apart a lot longer than they'd ever been together. "Whatever you want to do is fine with me."

Marilee hooked her arm through his and flashed him a smile from her pale, opaque green eyes. "May I hold you to that?"

His answering smile was only slightly forced as he disengaged his arm to open the door for her. "Why do I get the feeling that we're not talking about fishing?"

Her softly modulated laughter accompanied the sound of their descent of the wide wooden steps. Reaching the mossy brick walkway, Marsh turned instinctively toward the shady woods path. Marilee's ivory skin didn't take to the sun. She'd always looked after her complexion as conscientiously as she had her figure—as conscientiously as she had every single thing about herself, and it had paid off. He'd never seen her look less than perfect. But there were times when perfection could be so...

His thoughts homed in on the ring box in the corner of his suitcase. He'd bought the thing weeks ago, but then Tom had called him about this anniversary house party, and he'd decided to wait, hoping that some of the Gaillards' wedding bliss would rub off on them, maybe. Lord knows, they needed something to cancel out the taste of past mistakes—hers in marrying Kurtz, and his in allowing her to do it. He'd been furious, miserable, and then bitter when she'd run off with that gold-plated turkey. Then, last fall, when she'd come back single, he'd started seeing her again. They were more or less back at the starting point, he supposed—older and a little more wary. Just lately, she'd begun to hint at marriage. Ironically enough, it had roused a streak of stubbornness he hadn't even known he possessed. So maybe he was being too cautious—once burned and all that. Hell, he didn't know. He'd been hung up on the woman for so long now that he found it impossible to analyze his true feelings for her.

They sauntered along the winding path under the trees and came eventually to a wooden bench. Under a coat of pollen and lichens, numerous sets of crudely carved initials were still visible. He dusted off a place for Marilee to sit. Probably all the Gaillards—maybe the Abernathys, too, had taken a whack at immortality with a pen knife. Had Persia?

He had a mental image of her chubby little body crouched over with a knife, clumsily digging her initials in beside those of the older kids. He hadn't known her back then, but he'd lay odds that those remarkable eyes of hers hadn't changed all that much—nor her chin. The surface softness couldn't disguise that stubborn set.

A slow, sympathetic smile twisted his mouth as he pictured her in that godawful pink dress. She'd been odd man out at the wedding—young for her age and hopelessly outclassed by her cousin and Marilee. Poor child. Kathy'd been too excited to look after her, and Marilee had been too busy. Kathy had said her mother had died when she was thirteen, which was tough. That was bound to be a vulnerable age for a girl, and he had an idea that Persia had been far more vulnerable than most girls her age.

"—half a million for the house, and almost half that much for the property, and already erosion has eaten right up to the steps. Honestly, it's criminal!" Marilee rambled on about who among her friends had built beach places where.

Fortunately, answers were not required. The heavy sweetness of honeysuckle was lulling him into drowsiness again. In his mind, another voice, huskier, richer, overlaid Marilee's expensively acquired accent.

Persia. Where the dickens had she picked up a name like that?

She'd certainly turned out to be something else, hadn't she? The promise had been there all along, he supposed, under the puppy fat and the shyness. She'd more than lived up to it, too. Some man was going to land himself one hell of a good-looking woman. Some man probably already had, he amended with just the slightest twinge of dismay. An image of sweetly flared hips, full breasts and long, sleekly rounded thighs drifted before him, and he felt an uncomfortable stirring in his loins.

"Don't you think so?" Marilee asked.

"I expect so," he muttered absently.

"You expect—! Marsh, I told you, Freddie's broker said it was a sure thing. He called night before last—"

Marsh snapped his mind back on a leash and turned his attention to the woman beside him. "Sorry, Marilee, I've had a lot on my mind just lately. You were saying...?"

Chip Gaillard drove up in his vintage VW just as the others were sitting down to a dinner of fresh-caught bream and crappy. "Greetings, people," he called as he headed for the tiny bedroom off the kitchen, a canvas satchel in one hand and an attaché case in the other. "Be with you in a minute—don't wait."

Persia hadn't seen the younger Gaillard brother since her father's funeral, when Chip, surprisingly enough, had driven up from Atlanta to attend. He'd changed very little since their childhood, except for the moustache that adorned his thin, serious-looking face. He still wore the same Coke-bottle lenses in colorless plastic frames, the same—she could have sworn it was the *very* same—drab, tan-striped shirt with the cuffs turned back and the top button open. Chip was reportedly a "hot property" in the high-tech field. He'd had to fend off would-be employers before he'd even finished his second year at MIT.

"Now—what have we here? The usual plebian fare, I suppose—fried, boiled and stewed, respectively," he quipped as he slid into the place Kathy had hastily prepared for him. Glancing around, he nodded. "Marsh? How's the fourth estate these days? As biased as ever?" Not waiting for a reply, he turned his attention to Tom. "Big brother, still aspiring to be the king of torts, I suppose." Shifting his narrow body on the cane-bottomed chair, he managed to inject a degree or two of warmth in his voice. "Sister Katheryn—felicitations. I see you're still a disgrace to your liberated sisterhood." He nodded to the feast his sister-in-law had produced so lovingly and lavishly.

His thin lips twisted into a bitter smile as he turned to Marilee. "I understand congratulations are in order. In case my own esteemed wife asks, I'd take it as a personal favor if you wouldn't give her the name of the Shylock you sicced on poor old Freddie. Heard you took him to the cleaners, if you'll pardon the vulgar turn of phrase."

Tom reddened and opened his mouth to speak, but Kathy laid a placating hand on his arm. Chip hadn't changed. Persia braced herself for her own personalized greeting. Even so, she was unprepared for its crudity.

"Little Persia, I presume. How much did you lose? Fifty? Seventy-five? I always suspected there was a person under all that blubber."

Chairs scraped, and gasps came uniformly from around

the table. "You damned bastard!" Tom swore, and Kathy pulled on his arm when he would have jumped to his feet.

Even Marilee looked shocked, Persia noted numbly. Her own reaction was somewhat milder than the rest—probably because she'd sampled Chip's vicious tongue before. And oddly enough, his deliberate malice didn't bother her half so much as had Marilee's innocent cruelties. Some part of her that had long ago been tempered in a pretty hot fire recognized it for what it was Chip was hurting. For the first time it occurred to her that he, too, had been an outcast and a misfit all his life, if for a very different reason.

"It was closer to a hundred, actually," she told him, seeing the fixed look of stubborn misery on his bony face. "Only it was the same few pounds, over and over again. I think I'm the only woman in captivity who can actually gain weight on a reducing diet."

A collected sigh of relief arose from around the table. To cover any remaining awkwardness, Persia helped herself to another spoonful of coleslaw and passed the bowl to Tom, who passed it on to Marilee.

"Oh, heavens, no," she said in horrified tones. "Poor Persia's not the only one with a weight problem—I've gained two whole pounds just since I moved back to Columbia." She patted her twenty-two-inch waist and beamed at Marsh, and Persia could have throttled her quite cheerfully.

The talk, quite naturally, turned to diets, with Kathy and Marilee, sizes eight and six, respectively, leading the discussion. Persia opted out. She found the whole topic exceedingly boring. It was something one suffered in silence, not something one dragged up for dinner conversation.

"Have you caught any lunkers lately?" she asked Tom, shifting the talk to a subject she preferred. Actually, she would have preferred talking about the overgrown azaleas and camellias, the euonymous and eleagnus, and the pittosporum that banked the ancient brick foundation, but unless they'd changed drastically, there wasn't a gardening enthusiast in the bunch. She'd just have to wait to talk shop until she got back to Virginia.

At least the subject of weight and diet was out in the open now. She could refuse Kathy's rich desserts without having to be subtle. Munching absently on a strip of raw red cabbage, she frowned. It was Grandma Tat's coleslaw recipe, made with sour cream, lemon juice and honey. She might have known. Katheryn Abernathy—Tat to her family—had a lot of cholesterol and calories to answer for, bless her well-padded bones. She'd been dead for almost twenty years, but her sins lived on, in the form of a laboriously hand-written cookbook that had been copied by every branch of the family.

Persia stood and collected her plate as Tom reached for his pipe and Marsh took out a slender cigar. Chip, she noticed with a surge of sympathy, nibbled on a fingernail.

"What was this diet you gained weight on, Persia?" Kathy asked as she collected the silverware.

"Oh, it was just some high-fiber thing I read in a column in the paper," she dismissed, heading for the kitchen.

Marsh picked up his plate and iced tea glass and followed her out. "That wasn't by any chance a syndicated column called 'The High Road to Health,' was it?"

"Matter of fact, I think it was. Why?" She reached for Kathy's rubber gloves and frowned, laying them aside again. Her hands, while shapely enough, were the utilitarian sort. A little dishwater certainly wouldn't hurt them. Besides, the gloves were two sizes too small.

Marsh pursed his lips thoughtfully, and Persia, her eyes skittering away from his firm mouth, slammed the lid on her thoughts. Blowing a tendril of hair from her face, she twisted the faucet viciously, splashing the front of her silk shirt, and jumped back with an exasperated cry.

"I don't know if you're aware of it," Marsh said, reaching around her just as she jumped, to place his glass in the sink, "but I happen to own a few weeklies, and they all carry that particular column. I'd hate to think my professional reputation was at stake."

Trying valiantly to ignore the impact of the brief bodily contact, she eased aside, holding the sodden fabric away from her body. "Think what you like, it's the truth. I followed your damned diet and gained weight on it."

"I suspect you just forgot to—ah—take into account a few little snacks."

As Persia's hands moved to her hips, the wet silk fell clingingly to her breasts. She glared at him, her brown eyes snapping. "Are you saying I cheated?"

His mouth tilted in that characteristic downturned smile. "I didn't put it that way. I just said you forgot—"

"Forgot, hell! You think I cheated! You think I'm not capable of following a simple set of instructions."

"Now, Persia, calm down. I didn't mean anything by it, I was only—"

"You were only trying to save your precious professional pride at the expense of my—of my—"

The smile widened as his eyes were drawn to her shirt front. The thin wet fabric left little to the imagination. "Of your what? Honey, it's all right. I think you look terrific just the way you are."

"Don't patronize me, damn you. If I say I gained on your diet, then I *gained,* and you can just take your professional pride and stuff it."

Tom and Kathy collided in the kitchen doorway. "Hey, what's going on out here? Anybody need a referee?"

Kathy strode over to the sink, her brief tennis skirt switching around her doll-like hips. "Persia, I've got a dishwasher, for heaven's sake. You don't have to wash those things.''

Tom broke in anxiously, his homely-attractive face going from Marsh to Persia as they stood braced for battle. "I'm going to take the pontoon boat out for a little fishing. They ought to start hitting a surface plug just about dark. Anybody want to come along?''

Persia jumped at the chance to escape. "Give me two minutes to change out of these wet clothes, okay? Meet you down at the landing.''

Five minutes later, Persia took the steps two at a time, her eye on the blue and white striped canopy at the foot of the pier. If there was one thing she could do with right now, it was the soothing influence of a leisurely boat ride on a calm lake while the last of the lilac-colored sunset faded slowly from the sky. A little music would have been nice, too, but she doubted if Tom cared for background music when he was stalking the largemouth bass.

"Hi, I'm ready,'' she sang out as she slipped the cove hitch off the weathered old piling and prepared to lower herself under the canopy and into the aluminum boat. The lake was down considerably. All she could see from the high pier was one of Tom's sneakered feet and an open tackle box. Not until she ducked under the canopy did she see the extra set of feet, the extra pair of long, muscular legs.

In the far corner of the rectangular hull, Marsh was frowning as he sorted through a mess of tangled rigs held at arms length. He glanced up with a bland smile as her feet struck the carpeted aluminum deck.

"Hi, yourself. How's your close vision? Can you give me a hand with this stuff? I left my glasses up at the house.''

Tom was guiding the quiet outboard out onto the body of the lake before Persia could collect herself. "Shafted again," she muttered, picking her way past two open tackle boxes and one pair of worn white deck shoes. Taking a seat on the padded locker beside Marsh, she reached for the tangle of monofilament leaders, with their single shot weights and their triple-barbed Eagle Claw hooks.

Two sets of fingers worked at the snarled lines. Two sets of eyes studiously avoided meeting. Persia could feel the warm current of Marsh's breath on her neck as she bent her head over her task. "It's so blasted dark under here I don't know how anyone can expect to see," she grumbled.

"Here—pull on this, and I think we can cut these hooks free." Marsh proceeded to amputate two sets of hooks with his fishing knife. "I hope I didn't hurt your feelings back there, Persia," he said softly. "I wouldn't do that for the world."

"Nonsense," she said stiffly. "I've forgotten what we were even talking about. Are you going to use worms, minnows or artificial?"

He eyed her quizzically in the fast fading light. "A surface plug—maybe a Pie-eyed Piper. How about you?"

She shrugged, feeling a faint warmth from the day's dose of sun on her shoulders. "Why don't I run the boat while you two fish?"

Marsh leaned out to glance ahead of them. They were nearing a wooded point from which extended a long, narrow shoal. "Planning to anchor?" he called softly to Tom, who was steering with his elbow while he fed line off his reel.

"Hey, if you two don't mind," came the quiet reply, "I'd really like to get out here and try wading for bass. There's a lunker that hangs out just off the tip of this shoal—spooky old devil takes off the minute he hears anything. Take the boat on around the point, and I'll work my way around after I give him a few tries, okay?"

"Couldn't I...?" Persia's voice trailed off hopelessly. It was a small shoal, and in a case like this, one fisherman was enough. She was trapped as neatly as if Tom had planned it.

Marsh shifted his position so that he could take over the controls, and Persia shot him a resentful look. His gaze connected with hers in an open challenge, and she lifted her chin defiantly. He probably thought she was still upset by that childish business in the kitchen. He probably still saw her as a pudgy, adolescent who overdramatized everything. She was simply going to have to learn to handle it, that was all. And offhand, she couldn't think of a better way to exorcize old ghosts than to spend half an hour or so in an eight-by-sixteen-foot flatboat while Marsh bored her with tales of the big ones that got away. Fish, that was.

She moved to the bow and sat down facing him, her legs stretched out in front of her and her arms spread out along the shallow railing. *All right, Mr. Randolph the third—start talking, and I'll start watching all my old illusions disappear like so many pretty soap bubbles.* She'd seen too many stunning men lose their attractiveness the moment they opened their mouths. Unfortunately, she had a sneaking suspicion Marsh Randolph was not going to be one of them.

Marsh studied her thoughtfully as he steered the boat away from the long shoal, leaving Tom to his own devices. Somehow he'd managed to put himself in an awkward position, and it was going to take some nimble footwork to get himself out without bungling again. It hadn't occurred to him that she'd be sensitive about the fact that she was a large woman. Good Lord, didn't she realize how lovely she was? Still, he knew she'd probably had a rough time of it growing up. Kids could be hard on anyone who didn't fit the accepted standard. He'd have to watch it.

"Would you like to try for a striper?" he asked, tactfully shifting the focus from the personal. "They're probably still on the spawning run now. How'd you like to hook into a fifty-pounder—think you could handle it?"

Oh, hell, he'd goofed again. He could tell by the way she was looking at him that she'd taken a perfectly innocent remark all wrong. "Look, Persia, let's set the record straight, shall we? I did *not* imply that you cheated on your diet, and I was *not* hinting that a woman like you would only be interested in a trophy-sized fish."

"What do you mean, a woman like me? A brunette? A woman with pierced ears? A woman who wears flowered hats with jeans?"

Marsh swore with soft sincerity. Setting his jaw, he said, "Look, will you stop being so damned touchy? Did I interpret your remark about not being able to see as a personal slight just because I happen to wear glasses? Did I get steamed when you took a shot at a newspaper article? I *do* happen to be a newspaperman, you know."

"As a matter of fact," Persia said self-righteously, "You did. You accused me of—"

"I did not accuse you of anything! I merely said that you might have forgotten—"

Leaning forward, Persia planted her fists on her thighs and glared at him through the fading light. "There, now you're accusing me of being mentally deficient. You see? You can't open your mouth without making some personal remark."

"Ah *ha!*" Marsh glowered right back at her, but there was a suspicious twitch at the corner of his mouth. "Now who's making personal remarks? What did you mean by that crack, 'you see'? I could hardly even see the hooks on those damned leaders without my glasses, but do I let a simple phrase like 'you see' give me some sort of persecution complex? *Do I?*" he demanded, swinging the boat up toward a tiny, cypress-rimmed cove. His deep green eyes held hers captive until the soft scrape of a cypress knee against the hull broke the tense silence.

Persia crumbled first with a ladylike snort, and then with a gale of laughter. By the time he tilted the motor and shelved the boat on the sloping bank, Marsh was howling uninhibitedly. When he could get his breath again, he gasped, "There—see what I mean? There's no winning."

"Truce?" Persia offered, her lips still trembling with laughter.

"Truce. And before you dream up any more fancied insults, let me go on record as saying I think you're great."

She forced a scowl. "Great as in more than ordinary size?"

Marsh collapsed on the seat beside her, shaking his head. "No, lady—great as in gorgeous, ravishing, enchanting, alluring, terrific. Will that get me off the hook?"

"You really think on your feet, don't you?"

"Depends on what you call my feet," he retorted, settling himself more comfortably on the padded seat. Taking out one of his thin cigars, he asked permission to light it. "Might stave off the dive bombers you're attracting with your perfume. What is it, anyhow?"

"Something sinfully expensive with a French name I can't pronounce. My accent leaves a lot to be desired."

"So does mine," he murmured agreeably. "To my stepmama's chagrin. She tried to tutor me and gave it up as hopeless."

She glanced at him provocatively. "Oh? I would have thought you'd be a mean hand with a French menu."

"At least I know enough not to order snails. Actually, I can read the stuff well enough—I just can't wrap my vocal cords around my larynx enough to pass muster with a French waiter. They're a pretty supercilious breed."

Tilting her head, she studied his profile in the dim light that filtered through the lacy trees. "You're trying to make me believe you can be intimidated by a French waiter? Forget it.''

Stretching his arm along the railing, he extended his legs out across the blue carpeted cockpit. "Now, what on earth have I done in just a few hours to give you that sort of impression? I thought I'd been pretty docile.''

He'd be anything but docile if he had any idea how long he'd been simmering on the back burner of her mind. In her daydreams she'd used a lot of words to describe Marsh Randolph, but docile was not among them.

Instinctively veering away from treacherous grounds, she asked about his work. "You mentioned your weeklies—I take it you went into business with your father. He was in publishing, wasn't he?'' She caught a drift of fragrant smoke and inhaled deeply, catching nuances of sandlewood soap and healthy perspiration.

"Right. Regional magazines, mostly. He published the *Southern Exposure* and the *New South Review*, plus a couple of small quarterlies—literary and financial. He's retired now, lives in a small town in the Dordogne region of France.''

Tilting his head, he stared at a curl of smoke, and Persia waited for that deep, intriguing drawl to continued. *She was here! She was actually sitting here with Marsh Randolph, getting to know him as one adult to another.*

"The glossies didn't particularly interest me. A few years ago I had a chance to buy out a small publisher who was just this side of bankruptcy. In two and a half years I had three weeklies alive and well—circulation tripled and still growing. At the moment I'm in the middle of acquiring a Tennessee firm. If I can pull this one off, I'll have half a dozen publications over a three state area. If not, I reckon I'll be looking for a new trade.''

Not for one minute did she believe that. As the shadows flickered over the angular planes of his face, Persia had a fleeting impression of another Marsh Randolph—not the suave phantom lover she'd lived with for so long, not Tom's best friend and favorite fishing buddy—but a man who thrived on challenge. It was gone in an instant. Eyeing the relaxed figure in the comfortable, well-worn fishing clothes, she decided she'd been mistaken.

Marsh tossed the half-smoked cigar overboard and turned to her. "Didn't I hear something about your being in the gardening business?"

"That's one way of putting it—horticultural architect is a mouthful, and most people don't even know what it entails, anyway."

"Since I just paid a whopping big bill for the services of one, I happen to know. It was worth every penny. Amazing what clever planting can do to disguise a builder's mistakes."

"Imagine what it can do to enhance a showpiece—although I must admit, I'd rather tackle something a little more challenging. I did a job for a couple of garage owners who were being hassled by the zoning board. A conveniently placed trellis with a few fast growing vines, a dozen or so euonymouses, an eyecatching photinia hedge, and you'd never even notice all the wounded transmissions lying around."

"What made you get into that line of work?"

She shrugged, aware of a growing coolness now that the sun had gone. "I always had a green thumb—my one and only talent. I could root anything. I used to go along behind Hans, Daddy's gardener, and gather up the prunings, clip 'em here, clip 'em there, poke 'em in a bucket of wet, sandy soil and *voilà!* I don't think I ever lost a cutting. It compensated just a little for being so bad in so many other areas. I breezed through art, but believe me, nothing else came easy."

"Math was my *bête noir,*" Marsh confided. "English

was no problem, and I always liked geography, in spite of the fact that the text books were obsolete almost before we finished them.'' He laid a hand on her arm in a casual gesture. "Speaking of which, how the devil did you get a name like Persia? You weren't born there, were you?"

Shaken by the scalding warmth of his hand on her arm, Persia shook her head. Taking a deep breath she said, "Which version do you want? That I was conceived on an Oriental rug? Or my mother's famous quote, 'Iran out of gas halfway to the hospital, so Iran all the way there.' Believe me, I could have done with something a little less extraordinary.''

"Rough, huh? I took some ribbing about my name when I was a boy, too.''

"William?'' She sent him a puzzled look.

"Marsh. There were seventeen guys who thought it was short for marshmallow. Funny thing—every one of them happens to have a crooked nose.''

"A remarkable coincidence,'' she observed gravely.

His grin tugged downward, and Persia felt the old familiar pull of longing twist inside her. What *was* there about this one man? He wasn't even all that good-looking—at least, not in the traditional manner. There were lines crinkling about his deep-set eyes and shafting down his lean cheeks, his hair was about as tidy as a thatched roof, one of his teeth lapped ever so slightly over its neighbor. And she wanted to bury her face in his throat and breathe in the scent of him, savor the taste of his flesh, dig her fingers into the solid wall of muscles that bound his body. The sound of that deep drawl of his was like chocolate-covered gravel—she could drown in it.

"So you're in the landscaping business. Somewhere in Virginia, is that right?"

Bemused, she nodded. "Fredericksburg—just outside,

actually. It's nice country around there. Not quite so muggy as here.''

''Your work leaves you time enough for a pretty active social life, I suppose?''

''I suppose. Active enough, at any rate.''

He was pumping her in the most polite manner possible. He knew it; she suspected it, although she couldn't imagine why. ''I suppose you have to fight off men with a stick?'' he hazarded.

Blinking in amusement, she examined his tone for sarcasm and found nothing overt. Proceeding cautiously, she said, ''How flattering. But what makes you think I'd fight them off?''

He reached for her left hand and lifted it, examining the long, capable fingers with their neatly trimmed nails. ''No rings.''

''I'd hardly wear a ring fishing,'' she declared, impulsively making up her mind to use Patrick as a sop to her ego if need be. Patrick would hardly know the difference, and besides, he owed her that much.

''Then there is someone special?''

''Well, I could hardly spend *all* my time working,'' she parried. ''Anymore than you can. Are you and Marilee going to be here the whole two weeks?''

Carefully, he replaced her hand on her thigh and then he stroked his jaw thoughtfully. ''Lord, I hope so. I really need a break, but Marilee gets—restless.''

For restless, read bored, Persia thought sympathetically. Poor Marsh. If he tied himself down to a woman like Marilee, he could kiss his fishing days good-bye forever.

''So, what do you do when you're not designing landscape, Persia?''

''Nothing very spectacular, I'm afraid. I enjoy discovering new restaurants—I love dancing, and when I have the time and energy, I like to slip up to Washington and explore a new section of the Smithsonian.''

''Dining and dancing, hmmm? So there is someone special.''

She considered pleading the fifth amendment. It was either that or sound self-pitying, and whatever else she was, she was no wistful wallflower. *Sorry, Pat, but you do owe me one.*

''I suppose you could say Patrick's special. After all, I did agree to marry him,'' she evaded, trying for the Mona Lisa effect.

Patrick. Marsh examined the name and discovered he didn't care for it. He made a move to rise. ''Well, I guess we'd better get the anchor up while there's still enough light to locate it. Tom will be wading around the point any minute now. May as well go meet him—help hoist his lunker aboard.''

''Think so, huh? Without Kathy along, Tom's never caught anything larger than twelve inches, and in these waters, that's kindergarten stuff.''

''Are you a betting woman?''

''Only on a sure thing. Why? Would you care to place a small wager on his catch?'' Persia invited, lifting her head in an unconsciously provocative gesture.

''Two bits says he's got one over five pounds.''

''Two bits says he's got an empty stringer.''

''You're on,'' Marsh rejoined, his voice regaining some of the warmth that had been curiously absent for just a moment.

Chapter Three

Soon after Tom joined them on the screened porch after cleaning his single ten-inch bass, the conversation faltered again and died. Marsh and Persia had tacitly agreed that neither of them had won the bet. Marsh had joined the others, settling beside Marilee on the glider, and Persia had lingered inside to rummage in the refrigerator. She came out a few minutes later with a raw carrot and a glass of unsweetened iced tea.

By the time she finished both, Persia realized that, deliberately or not, Chip was blocking every attempt at conversation. Marsh mentioned an embassy incident that had recently been in the news, and Chip's gray eyes, hidden behind the thick lenses, riveted themselves to the speaker. When Tom assayed an answering remark, the gimlet gaze swung his way with the same silent intensity. Kathy and Marilee discussed fashions, and Chip focused his unwavering attention on each speaker in turn, as if the desultory conversation were a high-stakes tennis match, and he the scorekeeper. There were no more razor-edged remarks— no remarks at all. Just that disconcerting scrutiny from behind the thick lenses of his glasses. Intentional or not, he was killing any spark of conviviality before it had a chance to spread.

And I thought I was a social washout, Persia thought sympathetically. *Poor Chip hasn't a clue! No wonder Ann couldn't take it—how could any woman cope with a man who couldn't relax around ordinary mortals enough to make small talk?*

"How about a game of six-handed bridge?" she offered desperately when the silence had once more grown uncomfortable.

Chip, standing awkwardly in a corner with his hands clasped stiffly in front of him, muttered something about chess.

"Sorry, no chess board," Kathy answered apologetically. "How about Scrabble?"

Chip sent her a pained look. "Scrabble! Oh, okay. I'll play you in Latin or German—take your choice."

"No way," his sister-in-law wailed. "I can't even win in English!"

Persia sighed quietly. Poor little boy—play by his obscure rules or he'd take his marbles and go home. Standing up, she surveyed the small group brightly. "Hey, gang, how about a moonlight swim? Who's game? The air's cooled off a little, but the water'll feel as warm as milk."

Kathy jumped up and grabbed her husband by the hand, openly relieved at the last-minute rescue of her floundering house party. "Super! Come on, honey, we haven't done that in ages! Remember the last time?" She flashed a grin that on anyone but a tiny blue-eyed blonde would have been considered a leer.

Marsh looked up with a slowly widening smile, and

even Chip managed a mild show of interest. Before they could change their minds, Persia collared Chip and urged him into the house.

"Come on, Mr. Chips, climb into your trunks and I'll race you across to Piney Point. Drinks are on the loser."

"Oh, sure, you've got all that built-in buoyancy. It's all I can do just to stay afloat."

For once, there was no malice in his remark, and Persia wrinkled her nose at him as they split up in the living room. Chip headed for his downstairs bedroom and Persia hurried to her own room upstairs, congratulating herself on having saved the house party. It had been sinking fast, and here it was only the first night.

Actually, she'd been dying to go swimming all day. She'd invested in a knockout bathing suit—a coral and navy blue tropical print that nipped in her waist and flared out over her hips. Yanking it from her drawer, an unexpected surge of stage fright assailed her. *Ye gads, Persia, where's your brain? You can't go out there with a couple of pint-sized poster girls in bikinis—not with Marsh there to compare acreage.* With sagging spirits, she glanced out the small dormer that was set in the steeply sloping roof. It was almost ten—the moon was still hidden behind the clouds. From the porch below, a mumble of voices drifted up, and she sighed heavily.

She couldn't hide up here all night. Steeling herself, she shucked her clothes and pulled on the suit, taking time to braid her hair before facing the mirror. If she could just get over her first exposure, maybe the next time wouldn't be so bad. At least it was dark outside.

And the color really was scrumptious—it did marvelous things for her suntan. Pity she couldn't wear shoes in swimming. Ever since she'd discovered that the taller she stood, the slimmer she appeared, she'd fostered the illusion with platforms or skyscraper heels.

"Acres and acres of it, and all mine," she sighed, patting one of her round, honey-toned thighs.

Chip was waiting at the foot of the stairs. Minus his glasses, wearing a pair of boxer trunks that bunched out around his thin body, he looked pathetically pale and vulnerable, and Persia knew an unexpected surge of maternal warmth. She braced herself for his cutting comment, and when none was forthcoming, she smiled her relief and tucked a companionable hand in the crook of his arm. Underneath all that defensive spitefulness he was really rather sweet.

"Have fun," Marilee caroled playfully from the darkness of the screened porch. "In case we've gone up before you all get back, nighty-night."

"You all aren't coming with us?" Persia blurted, her disappointment only partially hidden.

"Darling, go have your fun—don't let us stop you, please," the older woman urged. "Marsh and I have lots to talk about, and besides, I never did care much for splashing about in a muddy pond."

"It's a lake, not a pond, and it's as clear as glass," Persia defended, feeling suddenly about as sophisticated as a wet puppy in the face of Marilee's polished savoir faire.

It had been a dumb idea in the first place, splashing around like a bunch of ten-year-olds! Of course, Tom and Kathy would be floating around together holding hands—they'd been doing it since high school days. Ten years of marriage didn't seem to have cooled them off all that much. And Marsh and Marilee would be sharing a glider and Lord knows what else on the shadowy, honeysuckle-scented porch. Which left the two misfits.

Oh, blast! When was she going to grow up? What good was a unilateral fantasy on a night like this? The idea of a moonlight swim had suddenly lost all its appeal, but she'd started the darned thing; she'd carry it off if it killed her. And knowing what was going on up here on the porch in the glider, it damned well might!

"Come on, Chip—last one off the pier is a deviled egg!" She caught Chip's hand and dashed down the steps and out across the front yard. By the light of the single bulb halfway along the pier, she could see Tom shifting the two boats out of the way so that they could dive off the end. Her footsteps slowed. She dropped Chip's hand and sighed unconsciously.

"Uh—Persia, about that race," Chip said with uncharacteristic hesitancy. "Maybe we'd better call it off. I'm not all that great a swimmer, and without my glasses, I'd probably wind up over the dam."

"Sure, no problem. I just want to swim a few laps so I can sleep. It's hard in a strange bed and all that," she offered dejectedly.

Standing at the edge of the porch, Marsh stared out at the shimmering reflections on the dark, still water and inhaled the resinous freshness of the night air. He'd excused himself to go inside and get a cigar. Now he stripped it, lighted it, and absently tucked the wrapper in his pocket. He'd caught a single glimpse of Persia as she'd passed under the pier light before she'd been swallowed up by darkness. The image of a thick black braid centering her tanned back swam before his eyes and faded again as he fingered his cigar thoughtfully. He hoped she knew what she was doing—night swimming was not without its hazards.

At least Chip wouldn't be one of them...or would he? Sending out a stream of blue smoke to repel the invading insects, Marsh considered the younger Gaillard brother. He was reputed to be a brain, which was fortunate, because he certainly didn't have much else going for him. Actually, he wasn't bad looking, if one cared for the studious, undernourished type. In fact, he'd probably be the sort to stir up all kinds of protective, maternal feelings in certain women…women like Persia, for instance, who happened to be warm and open and generous by nature.

Drawing fiercely on the rich tobacco, Marsh was conscious of a feeling of irritation. He hoped to hell she'd have the common sense not to get herself involved in the boy's problems. If disposition was anything to go by, he was in a bad way—his wife had walked out on him just a few weeks ago, according to Tom. Marsh could almost remember the fine edge of rage and frustration he'd felt when Marilee had run off with Kurtz without even bothering to let him know. At this stage of the game, the poor devil would be down on all women. His inexcusable performance at dinner tonight had been tolerated only for that reason.

Still, he and Persia seemed chummy enough now. Poor guy was following her around like a homeless mutt, looking for a nice soft bosom to unload his troubles on. It could spell trouble for both of them. He was vulnerable and she was far too easygoing.

Marsh stubbed out the cigar in a flowerpot. Damn it, the boy already had a wife, and Persia had herself a man— and if this Patrick fellow up in Virginia wasn't smart enough to keep her in line, he deserved to lose her. All the same, Marsh determined, he'd keep an eye on her—as a favor to her cousin Kathy, if for no other reason. He thought the world of Kathy and Tom. He and Tom had been friends since they'd roomed together at U.S.C. He'd hate like the devil to see anything happen to mar their anniversary party.

His grim thoughts were interrupted by Marilee's soft voice. "Aren't you finished with that smelly old thing yet? Darling, why don't you pour us both a glass of wine, and we'll go upstairs. I haven't even finished unpacking yet, and I do want your opinion of the dress I bought for the dance.''

It was the sort of invitation a man would have to be crazy to turn down. Aware of an odd restlessness, Marsh shrugged away from the pillar and opened the screened door. Marilee was waiting for him. She leaned against him delicately, lifting her face for his kiss.

"Ugh, you smell like cigars! I thought you only smoked when you had something on your mind.''

"What makes you think I don't?" he teased, forcing his mind away from the laughter and splashing out beyond the reach of the pier light.

"You promised me you were going to forget all about business so that we could enjoy ourselves.'' She sent him a pouting look under a fan of dense black lashes, and Marsh shifted uncomfortably under an inexplicable attack of guilt.

"Is that an offer?" Wrapping an arm around her slender back, he led her inside.

A small, cynical voice whispered from a corner of his mind that the only real emotion he'd seen any evidence of was her reaction to the collapse of one of her tax shelters. Surprisingly enough, he was just now coming to realize that that cool beauty of hers hid an even cooler brain. He'd been so struck by her looks when Tom had first introduced them that it had taken him a long time to look further. Lately, though, he was beginning to wonder just where her greatest interest lay—in the bedroom or in the boardroom.

Marilee glanced up at him expectantly as he paused outside her door. "Aren't you coming in?"

His mind flashed to the two-carat emerald with its frame of diamonds that was nesting securely in his suitcase. This would be as good a time as any to make it official. "The others will be trooping in any minute now," he heard himself saying hesitantly. "Maybe we'd better—"

"I only wanted to show you my dress," she snapped. "Are you afraid of being compromised?"

Turning her to him, Marsh lifted her chin and gazed down into her angry eyes. Even in anger they were cool. Pale, strikingly lovely, but...

The image of a pair of brown eyes dancing with amber lights intruded, and with a soft oath he lowered his head and took her mouth in a fierce kiss. The taste of her lipstick was vaguely medicinal, the scent of the perfume he'd given her, suddenly repellant. Grinding his mouth against hers in baffled frustration, he felt her stiffen in his arms. He eased his grip, despising himself for using the advantage of his superior strength against anyone so small and delicate. He was in a rotten mood, but there was no point in taking it out on Marilee.

"I'm sorry, honey—it's not you, it's me. I guess it's just been a long day, and I've been putting in too many eighteen-hour ones lately. Rain check?" Remorsefully, he watched as she patted her hair back to its usual smoothness, peering around his shoulder to see into the hall mirror. He'd smudged her lipstick; he was probably wearing as much of it now as she was.

Marilee touched her lips delicately with her little finger. "Oh, look at me—I look positively debauched."

Debauched? It was the last word he'd ever have used to describe her. Crossing his arms over his chest, he leaned against the wall and waited until she'd repaired the evidence of his assault. A subliminal vision flashed before his eyes: a richly tanned face, cheeks flushed from equal amounts of sun and passion, naked lips parted and blatantly hungry.

"There—that's better. Now come in and let me show off my dress. You'd die if I told you how much I paid for it, but it was worth every dollar." Turning into her room, she opened the closet door and took out a gleaming creation of stiff blue and green taffeta. "Of course, it's much too much for that dinky little club of Tom's, but I couldn't resist. Will I make an impression on the locals, do you think?" She uttered a small, disdainful laugh. "When I bought it, I had something slightly more romantic in mind. Neil Diamond and lobster Bordelaise instead of the Peach Wine Ramblers and catfish stew."

"You'll manage," Marsh assured her. "The dress is beautiful. You'll be the belle of the ball in it."

Holding it in front of her, Marilee pirouetted before the mirror. "That's no great achievement, considering the competition." Catching his expression, she added hastily, "Oh, not Kathy, of course—but then, she's hardly competing, is she? Honestly, those two are unbelievable. Imagine, after all these years they've got nothing better to do than drift around in a smelly old boat and catch slimy old fish. Kathy used to be fairly good company, but marriage has ruined her. As a hostess, she spends all her time in the kitchen, and when she finally gets out, she goes fishing."

"She's happy," Marsh reminded her dryly. "Don't knock fishing until you've tried it. It can serve as either a stimulant or a tranquilizer, depending on your particular needs—not to mention putting some pretty fine meat on the table."

Spreading the dress carefully across the foot of her bed, Marilee raised her arms and began playfully walking her fingertips around his shoulders. "Don't be cross with me, darling," she pouted prettily. "I was only teasing. Honestly, I think it's sweet the way Tom and Kathy enjoy such simple little pleasures. And as for fishing—did I tell you about the place Sonja and Carl Mitiver bought at Figure Eight? Carl keeps his yacht there, and Sonja says he supports a Florida taxidermist single-handedly—they've even got trophies mounted in the servants' quarters."

Marsh rested his forehead against her hair. How could

anything look so incandescent and feel so cool to the touch? He had a sudden urge to break through the laquered perfection and tousle it with his hands, but he resisted it. She wouldn't thank him, and besides, he acknowledged reluctantly—it might lead to something he wasn't really in the mood for.

"I think I'll take a quick dip, after all," he murmured against the cool skin of her throat. He had to bend at an awkward angle to reach her, and he tried to ignore the catch in his back. Now he knew why some men put their women on a pedestal—it was the only way to get to them. "A swim might help me get some sleep."

Easing away from his arms, Marilee leaned back to smile at him. "I did offer to help ease your insomnia, darling, but if you really prefer swimming…"

He'd forgotten the insomnia bit. Actually, he'd had trouble sleeping just lately—since he'd started seeing Marilee again, as a matter of fact. Unfortunately, it wasn't the sort of insomnia that responded to cold showers. He could have dealt with that sort of thing easily enough, one way or the other.

"See you in the morning, honey," he said softly, kissing her lightly on the tip of the nose. He kept forgetting how it annoyed her, and now he laughed apologetically as she brushed away the touch of his lips.

Entering his own room a moment later, Marsh hurriedly peeled his shirt over his head. When Tom had asked tactfully how many rooms he'd be needing, he'd mentioned the trouble he'd been having with insomnia. "Better give me a single if you've got it," he said. "No point in keeping anyone else awake." If Marilee had been surprised, she'd hidden it well enough. Nor had she registered any great degree of disappointment. She was a fastidious little lady at all times, and he had an idea that bedroom games in someone else's house wasn't precisely her style.

He pulled on his trunks, snatched up a towel from the bath on his way out, and closed the screened door quietly behind him. An unexpected feeling of anticipation sparkled through his bloodstream as he loped across the dark yard toward the pier.

They were coming in. Disappointment slammed into his solar plexus as he watched her strolling up the boardwalk, laughing that rich, clear laugh of hers at something one of them had said. Even barefooted, she was an inch or so taller than Chip. Poor little Kathy faded into insignificance beside her Junoesque cousin.

"Oh, hi," Persia greeted him. Her smile had wavered only briefly when she'd caught sight of him a moment earlier. She paused while the others hurried by, arguing about who was going to shower and who was going to have another serving of cake. "Decided to swim after all? Where's Marilee?"

"I left her upstairs in her room." He was glaring at her angrily, totally unaware of doing so. Persia winced imperceptibly and shrugged her wetly gleaming shoulders. As she brushed past him to catch up with the others, he caught the clean scent of lake water and a hint of that elusive perfume of hers. It made the scent his secretary had picked out for Marilee's birthday seem cloying, and for some reason, that irritated him enormously.

He went off the end of the pier, his momentum carrying him some distance before he surfaced. For perhaps five minutes he swam furiously, and then he rolled over onto his back and stared up at the night sky, his thoughts returning to a certain large, lovely, and inexplicably exasperating woman.

"Not grits and gravy again, *puh-lease,*" Persia groaned. Tom had already finished, and Chip was digging into a plate of fried eggs, country ham, grits and red-eye gravy. "That's really hitting below the belt, Kathy."

Chip eyed the soft curve of her stomach in the oyster linen slacks. "Literally," he quipped.

Snaring a chair, she sat down beside him and grimaced. "Look who's talking. You can eat like a platoon of Hussars and never gain an ounce. People like you should be outlawed."

"Oh, I'm overweight, too—it's just that it's in a place where it doesn't show—my brain."

"Kathy, do you think Tom would mind if I used his baby brother for fish bait?" Persia turned a plaintive look on her cousin, who was ladling a large spoonful of gravy onto a mound of grits. "Hey, if that's for me, forget it. I may not have a fat head, like some people I could mention, but if I gain another ounce I won't be able to squeeze into my knock-'em-dead outfit next Saturday night."

Marsh's soft-soled deck shoes silenced his approach. Persia started as he pulled out a chair and sat down beside her, resting his arm on the table beside hers... "I'll take it, Kath—a glass of water and a heel of bread for my friend here," he ordered imperiously.

"Bread!" Persia snorted. "That shows how much *you* know about dieting."

"Oh, so we're back to that, are we? Okay—you're a betting woman, I'm a betting man. Last night's little wager turned out to be a dud, but how about this one? You go on a legitimate reducing diet for one week. If you actually gain so much as an ounce, you win. If you lose—even an ounce—I win. Fair enough?"

Persia shoved her chair out and stood up, needing to put some distance between them in case she succumbed to a violent urge to run her palm over the crisp, sun-bleached hair that glistened on his muscular arm. "Whoa. Back up a bit—what legitimate diet are you talking about? Fasting?

Scarsdale? Cambridge? Beverly Hills? Sure, I'll lose a few pounds of water weight, but in a matter of days I'll gain it back again, plus a few extra pounds.''

"I was talking about the one you found in my paper."

"It wasn't your paper, it was the *Rappahannock Banner*."

"Same thing—we all carried the column." Marsh reached for another slice of fried country ham and slid an egg off the platter onto his plate.

Persia's stomach growled. She watched while he broke the semisoft yolk and let it swim under a bite of ham before he lifted the fork to his mouth. She followed every movement of his freshly shaven jaw as he chewed slowly and appreciatively. Under the supple covering of tanned skin, the muscles of his throat worked smoothly, and he favored her with a benign smile as he reached for another French biscuit—made with butter *and* lard, as Persia well knew.

"Pass the watermelon preserves, will you, Chip?" Glancing up at where Persia stood, her teeth clenched impotently, he said, "Well?"

"You think I can't do it, don't you?"

Kathy broke in with the offer of a plain boiled egg, and Persia ignored her. "You think I can't watch the rest of you all making pigs of yourself over Grandma Tat's recipes, and still stick to a diet. Well, if you can find that diet in one of the old magazines in the living room then I'll stay on it for seven days and come off weighing more then I did when I started!" she challenged rashly.

She knew perfectly well she was making a mistake, but she was constitutionally unable to refuse a dare. Just look at him—smirking at her like a tomcat with his whiskers full of cream, daring her to take him up on it. It wouldn't be the first time her impulsive nature had got her in trouble, and it wouldn't be the last, but at least this time she

cate just the right shade of carpet for your gameroom, Marilee.''

She caught Chip's eye as he hunched over his mug of coffee, and he shook his head at her. ''Naughty, naughty,'' he mouthed silently, and Persia ducked her head, hiding her smile.

The day was endless. Kathy and Marilee drove into North Charleston after lunch to shop for a pair of sunglasses—Marilee hadn't been able to find what she wanted in Moncks Corner. Morosely, Chip dug out his briefcase. It turned out to be a personal computer, and he was soon lost in the intricacies of a language Persia had never even heard of. From time to time, he glanced up to frown absently at the phone. In the far corner of the room, Tom whistled tunelessly around the stem of his pipe while he sanded and revarnished a split bamboo fly rod. Persia, under Marsh's tender, solicitous supervision, starved.

She dusted the living room and mopped the kitchen and made her bed. Then she emptied the dishwasher, eyeing the clock desperately as the hands inched slowly toward the next mealtime.

Nor was it all that worth waiting for. Prowling restlessly around the house after a skimpy dinner, she tried to ignore Marilee's gleaming head hovering over Marsh's as she sat on the arm of the couch and leaned over to point out something in a paper he was reading. At the sound of her soft, well-bred laughter, Persia slammed down the book she'd just picked up.

''Hungry, dear?'' Marilee glanced up at her sympathetically. ''I've always heard dieting makes some women irritable, but it's for a good cause. You have such a pretty face—just think how marvelous you'll look minus all those extra pounds.''

''I'm not being irritable,'' Persia snarled. ''Dieting

might make me weepy, but there's nothing at all wrong with my disposition!''

From his chair in the corner of the room, Chip entered the fray. "Let me know if you're planning to get any happier, Persia—I want to take cover."

"Children, children," Kathy soothed, and Persia's annoyance evaporated.

"Sorry," she mumbled with a reluctant giggle. Surprisingly, it was Chip who joined in, his laughter sounding as if it had been packed away for years.

Marsh laid aside his paper and took off his glasses, rubbing the bridge of his nose tiredly. "Tom—care to join me on the porch for one last smoke?"

"Oh, must you? I thought we might go out and sit in the glider for a while," Marilee crooned softly.

A smothering gray gloom descended on Persia again, and rather than inflict her moodiness on the others, she said a short goodnight. The first day of a diet was apt to be filled with emotional squalls. Once her stomach got the message that she meant business, her brain would settle down.

She couldn't sleep, of course. The sheets felt like rumpled canvas after she'd tossed for several hours, and in desperation, she stood up and took off her gown and flung it aside. With all her twisting and tossing, it had turned into a straight jacket. Bias-cut satin and Chantilly lace! What the devil had she been thinking of when she'd put down sixty-nine ninety-five for that silly bit of nonsense?

The question was not what, but who. Resignedly, she faced facts. She knew who she'd been thinking of, and it hadn't been Patrick Blake, either. With an irritated gesture, she tossed off the suffocating weight of the percale sheet and got up again to prowl the confines of her small room. She was tired. She was restless, too. It was too hot to sleep.

Maybe she'd better cut her losses and get the devil out of here. There was nothing to be gained by staying. Meeting her fantasy head-on had certainly not proved anything—except, perhaps, that she had even better taste in men than she'd realized.

Taste. She was *hungry*. That's what was wrong—she was starving! He *would* have to pick out that particular diet. She'd been on a modified version of it several years ago, and she knew that it wasn't going to do her any long-term good. Three pounds the first twenty-four hours, three-quarters of a pound a day for the next four days, and then nothing. Zilch. She could threaten the scales with a crowbar and they wouldn't drop another ounce. Her own plateau always came disgustingly early in the game, and it took forever to start losing again.

Downstairs in the kitchen there was a cannister of pecan pralines, half a Lady Baltimore cake, some leftover Hopping John, and two cold fried chicken backs. She'd go down and have herself a large glass of ice water.

Slithering her gown on over her head again, Persia cracked the door and listened for a moment before tiptoeing out on the landing. It had to be long past midnight. She'd been turning and tossing for hours. The first day of a diet was always this way—she was obsessed by the idea of food. Normally, she got by well enough with her old standbys—eggs poached in tomato juice, enormous salads, broiled fish and chicken, and steamed vegetables. She was usually too busy to be hungry, but just let her start on a new diet and her whole system went haywire. The munchies nearly drove her out of her mind.

The fluorescent light over the kitchen range was enough to see by. Piously averting her face from the sideboard where the cake stand was enshrined, she took down a glass and poured herself some cold water. Sipping it slowly, she leafed through the evening paper someone had left on the table. Only after she'd scanned the gardening page and read her favorite comic strip did she saunter casually over to the sideboard. Speculatively, she eyed the tall, copper-domed cake stand. It couldn't hurt just to look at it. Nobody actually gained weight from just *looking* at a cake, regardless of what she'd often suspected.

Her hand hovered over the cover as she visualized the light, almond-flavored cake with its fig and raisin and nut frosting. Her finger had no more than touched the cool metal surface when the overhead light flared on, and she jumped, sending her water glass crashing to the floor.

"Damn it, what are you trying to do, scare me to death?" She plucked the dripping tea-rose satin away from her thighs and glared at the intruder, her pulse rate accelerating still further as she took in his haystack hair and the broad expanse of his bare chest.

"More to the point, what are *you* doing?" Marsh challenged. "Don't move—I'll get a broom and clear up the broken glass."

Neatly trapped, Persia huddled in the corner by the giant oak sideboard, the cake forgotten in light of the current crisis. She watched in helpless embarrassment as Marsh swept the shards into a dustpan and tipped them into the trash. He turned back to where she stood, scanning the floor around her bare feet.

"Hold it—I think I see something shining by your left heel." He knelt beside her, his head pressing against her knee, and then he stood up and brandished a vicious sliver of glass. "Got it. You ought to wear slippers when you sneak down here to raid the refrigerator."

"I did *not* sneak down her for that," she declared peevishly.

"A technicality. I caught you red-handed. Care to explain what you were doing by the cake stand?"

She grimaced at the clammy feel of the wet satin. Was

she destined to be drenched every time she got close to him as retribution for her old sins? "I was just going to look at it," she informed him haughtily.

"Just going to *look* at it," Marsh echoed disbelievingly. "Now I've heard everything!"

"Oh, don't be such a—" Starvation always affected her tear ducts first. Sniffling, she tried to sidle past him.

He blocked her escape with a hand on her shoulder. "Persia? Honey, what's wrong? If you're really hungry, why don't you have something—have a slice of cake. Hell, no silly diet's worth all this much grief."

"I'm not hungry," she wailed, holding her gown away from her body as far as the fitted design would permit. She was beyond worrying about modesty—he could have seen far more of her last night in her bathing suit if he'd bothered to look. "I only wanted a glass of water—I couldn't sleep, and I—"

"I know, I know," he murmured soothingly. He was still holding the sliver of glass, and turning, he tossed it into the trash. "I have trouble sleeping sometimes, myself. Warm milk helps, I've heard. Want to give it a try?" His smile, downturned corners and all, was ineffably sweet, and she felt herself sinking under the mixture of potent virility and genuine concern. He was wearing the white rugby pants instead of pajamas, and she wondered fleetingly if he slept in the raw.

"With a little bit of chocolate syrup in it?" she asked wistfully.

"Sure, why not?"

"No, I don't think so," she sighed. "I'm not about to forfeit our bet just because my stomach thinks my mouth's left town."

His shadowy gaze traced her features. "You're sure? You know you really don't need to lose any weight. You look fine just the way you are."

Eyes brimming with the quick tears she was prone to, she countered his assurances. "You mean I look fine for a fat person."

Marsh's brows lowered swiftly. He reached out to catch her arms in a painful grip. "No, damn it, I did *not* mean that! I meant exactly what I said—you look fine. In fact you look lovely—beautiful—glowing—what else can I say?"

Reeling from the intoxicating force of his nearness, Persia blinked at the angular face that was only a few inches above her own. "Well, you can stop patronizing me, for starters. And you can stop trying to chicken out of our bet. We never got around to naming the stakes, but I want you to know you're not going to get off easy. I'm going to make you pay dearly for doubting my integrity."

A vibrant mixture of emotions seemed to hover between them. Persia trembled between tears and laughter as serrated nerves gouged her to new heights of recklessness. She could feel his fingers digging deeply into her tender flesh, his breath making warm sweet currents on her overheated face.

And then, gradually, his hands eased their pressure and began moving in a slow, hypnotic pattern. "Just for the record, I meant every word I said, Persia. Don't ever—*ever* underestimate yourself." His voice fell softly on her ears, causing the crystalline web of her emotions to tremble dangerously.

Dropping his hand as if he'd just noticed its whereabouts, he said, "As for backing out on our bet, I wouldn't dream of it." His eyes gleamed wickedly. "I'm already calculating how much this is going to cost you."

"Don't count your chickens," she jeered, and then, with a sigh that came from the depths of her hungry soul, she whispered, "Chicken. Fried in benne seed batter. There are two crispy fried backs left, and a bowl of Hopping

John—and unless those sharks ate the last of it, there's half a cake under here.'' Reverently, she touched the lid to the cake stand. ''And I can't have *any* of it,'' she wailed. ''And if you think I'm going to stand here and watch while you—''

He shook her gently. ''Hey—how about a refreshing glass of ice cold water, hmmm?'' Taking down another glass, he filled it from the container in the refrigerator and held it out to her.

''I'm not thirsty.''

''Come on—this one's on me.'' He glanced down at the tissue-thin silk that clung to her thighs like a second skin, and grinned irreverently. ''At least it's not pink. It won't stain your gown.''

Spontaneous laughter bubbled forth, jarring a single tear from its precarious perch as Persia's emotions took still another erratic swing. ''Oh, you wretch! I'd hoped you'd forgotten about that.''

He shook his head, reaching out a finger to catch the tear as it traced a crooked downward path. ''You cry as easily as you laugh, don't you?''

Sensing danger of a sort she wasn't equipped to deal with, Persia moved away and managed a semblance of a smile. ''Do me a favor and ignore it, will you? I promise you, it doesn't mean a thing. When I'm hungry I always get emotional. Three days on a tough diet and I could cry over a bent license plate.''

Marsh's gaze wandered searchingly over her face. ''Drink your water,'' he commanded gruffly. He leaned against the cabinet and watched while she lifted the glass and drank. His eyes flowed over every inch of her, returning to the area where her gown tucked under the rich curve of her breasts. Swallowing hard, he wrenched his eyes away, fastening them instead on the hands that held the tumbler.

"Still no ring, huh?" he taunted gently. "You're not fishing now."

No ring? Puzzled, Persia stared at him, and then she remembered. "I—I never wear jewelry to bed."

His eyebrows lifted skeptically. As his gaze lingered on the moisture glistening on her lips, he felt an uncomfortable tightness growing inside him, and he shifted his position restlessly. "Tell me about him, Persia," he invited, needing something to disrupt the unexpected turn his thoughts had taken.

Of all the topics he could have introduced, that was one she could have done without. "What do you want to know? His name is Patrick Hamilton Blake, and he's a very successful lawyer, and I knew his sister at Mary Washington. The family goes back to the year one. Their blood, according to rumor, is somewhere between cobalt and ultramarine."

And her own was decidedly red—which, along with certain other traits, had made her totally ineligible for the position of Mrs. P. H. Blake. After all, the man would someday be governor of Virginia, if his mother had anything to do with it, and it would never do to have a governor's wife who might be tempted to set up a fruit and vegetable stand on the front lawn of the governor's mansion.

"So—and what's your blue-blooded boy friend doing while you're lolling about here in Pinopolis?"

Doing exactly what Mommie tells him to do, Persia thought with a surprising lack of dismay. "If he's got any sense at all, he's in bed asleep," she said shortly. "And now, if you'll excuse me…"

"Then he can thank me later for filling in for him," Marsh said, capturing her neatly and pulling her against him. "No woman should have to go to bed unkissed."

Chapter Four

It was over almost before she could react, the incredibly soft brush of his mouth against hers. He released her and she stepped back, staring at him with something akin to wonder.

And then she caught herself up and bolted from the room, not pausing until she was safely barricaded behind her bedroom door.

Experimentally, she touched her lips in an effort to recapture the feel of his kiss. It had been a mere whisper of a kiss—soft as dandelion down. The sort of kiss one gives a child—only Marsh was no child, and neither was she.

Hunger was forgotten as Persia lay on her back and stared up at the streak of moonlight that angled across the sloping ceiling over her bed. She'd fantasized about his kisses for years, only how could she have imagined that his lips would feel like that? Like warm, moist velvet— like butterfly wings. That firm, almost stern mouth, with the wry twist, had hovered over hers for no more than a split second, and she was marked indelibly for life.

For several minutes Marsh stood in the doorway of the kitchen staring at the fading after-image. It occurred to him belatedly that someone might have heard their voices. The crash of the glass had been enough to rouse the household. Persia, he mused...little Persia Abernathy. God, he'd better get a grip on himself. All sorts of wild, unlikely notions were beginning to hatch out in his brain. If he didn't watch it, he'd be upsetting Marilee, and then he really would be in trouble. Marilee didn't care for competition. Not that she'd seriously consider Persia competition.

Hell, she was little more than a child—she was at least ten years younger than any of the rest of them. She was barely out of her teens. He'd already had his thirty-sixth birthday. Persia was—what? Twenty-two? No, more like twenty-four or -five by now, but somehow, he still thought of her as the child she'd been when he'd first seen her.

Who was he kidding? That was no child he'd held in his arms just now, no child who'd wandered in and out of his thoughts at the drop of a hat ever since he'd arrived, with no respect at all for his peace of mind. Tonight he'd finally given up and come downstairs for a cup of coffee, figuring that if he was going to have to stay awake, he might as well do a thorough job of it and get some work done.

Only his briefcase was upstairs, and she'd been downstairs, and suddenly he hadn't given a damn about circulation problems in Hartsville, or a transplanted California editor in Florence who was homesick for the West Coast.

"Marsh? Is that you?" Marilee called softly from the foot of the stairs. "I thought I heard someone down here. What's wrong?"

Running a hand through his hair, he brushed away the

remnants of the past few minutes and snapped off the light. "Nothing, honey—sorry I disturbed you."

"I'm not sorry, darling. If you need me, you know I'm only too happy to do what I can. What about some warm milk?"

Stiffling an uncharitable thought, Marsh shook his head. "No problem. I'll be all right now." He wondered briefly if it was fair to ask one woman to put out a fire started by another one.

The first two days of any diet were the worst, Persia consoled herself as she savored the almondlike flavor of the last seed of her mid-morning apple. On second thought, yesterday's breakfast had been easy. She'd come downstairs late to find Marsh alone in the kitchen. The others had already finished and were scattered about the house.

"Morning," he'd greeted her with an annoyingly irresistable smile. "Got it all ready for you. One serving fruit, your choice—banana today, okay? One slice unbuttered whole-wheat toast, and one cup black coffee."

Stubbornly ignoring him, Persia had wandered over to the back door to stare unseeingly out at what had once been an herb garden. Sooner or later she was going to have to round up some gardening tools and have a go at it.

"Persia?"

"I'm really not very hungry," she'd snapped. And illogically enough, it had been true. She'd had to force down every single bite, and with Marsh beaming down at her like an indulgent uncle, cheering her on, it was a wonder she hadn't choked.

It had been the same at lunch yesterday, with him filling her plate with a spoonful of lowfat cottage cheese and an assortment of raw vegetables. To her chagrin, he'd made a special trip to Moncks Corner for the cottage cheese.

"Lemon or vinegar?" he'd inquired in a ludicrous imitation of a French waiter.

She'd relented, finally, and waded through the bushels of shrubbery that were allowed on the diet. By dinnertime, after an afternoon of wondering where Marsh and Marilee had gone in his car, she'd been so mopy she'd almost skipped dinner. Marsh had returned in time to rinse all the loose calories from her shrimp, and she'd munched them despondently, along with her usual salad, while everyone else enjoyed them simmered in highly seasoned broth, laced with butter and vinegar, and served on a bed of rice. And the worst part of it all was that she hadn't even cared about the food—she'd simply felt disheartened. Watching Marsh and Marilee's heads together as they laughed at some bit of nonsense, she'd felt a mixture of loneliness and frustration. One thing was certain—she'd never crave another M & M!

Today had been a little better. She was not normally a morose person, and after a breakfast of cantaloupe, toast and coffee, she'd spent the morning weeding the brick-edged garden plot. The soil was rich and loamy, but the trees had gotten so large that scarcely any sun reached the backyard anymore. Maybe she'd put in a rock garden, a few squares of sansevieria and caladium, brick in a few walkways and a section in the center for a picnic table and...

Good Lord, she was only here for another week and a half. Besides, the place wasn't hers, and neither Tom nor Kathy had expressed any interest in the landscaping at all.

Dusting her grimy hands on the seat of her shorts, she let herself in the back door just as the others were assembling for lunch.

"Oh, Persia!" Marilee groaned. "What on earth have you been up to? Making mud pies?"

A spark of amusement lit Persia's damp, exertion-flushed features. "I'm not quite that desperate." Winking at Chip, she ambled toward the downstairs washroom, trying hard to ignore the rich aroma that was being wafted about by the lazy blades of the ceiling fan. Chicken soup. Ten to one it was Tat's white soup, made with a pint of whole milk and a quart of cream—not to mention the bread, the flour and a nice, fat hen.

"Kathy, you shouldn't have," Marilee was saying when Persia rejoined the others.

"Kathy, you *really* shouldn't have," Persia echoed feelingly. "Are you trying to test my willpower?"

Ladling up the rich cream soup, Kathy looked up innocently. "Well, what do I know about reducing diets? I've weighed the same since I was thirteen years old."

"You're not supposed to spend your whole vacation in the kitchen," Persia pointed out, accepting the usual plate of assorted raw vegetables from Marsh. She looked up to meet his commiserating grin. "And neither are you, Marsh. Is this your idea of fun? Hacking innocent little vegetables to death?"

"*I* hacked your innocent vegetables," Kathy retorted. "I doubt if Marsh would know a cauliflower from a caterpillar."

"Yikes! And this is the man I trusted to dole out my rations? Marsh, are you sure there's not just a tiny bit more protein on this plate than the law allows?"

"If it has bristles on it, spit it out," Marsh ordered, seating Marilee and then taking his place between her and Persia. "All I do is measure and see that you get exactly sixteen ounces of the proper calories per meal, but if Kath's complaining about doing double duty, then I assure you, I can take over the full preparation. In fact, I'm beginning to enjoy learning my way about the kitchen. For instance, I never realized that there was a life after death for newspapers—and here I thought their usefulness ended once the crossword was finished.''

Marilee toyed with her spoon and took a sip of water. She disdained both coffee and tea on the grounds that they were reputed to be harmful to the complexion. ''I knew it would come to this,'' she intoned. ''Not only do we have to eat in the kitchen—we have to discuss every tedious little calorie as if it were the most fascinating subject on earth. Honestly, do you people realize how deadly dull your conversation is? No one with any breeding discusses reducing diets—it's hopelessly declassé.''

Chip, who had spent the morning pacing the shoreline like a lost soul, swiveled his head to stare at her. Collective breaths were caught and held as they awaited his cutting rebuttal. When, without having spoken a word, he turned his attention back to his soup, a soft sigh of relief drifted around the table. Actually, there had been no more outrageous remarks from him since that first night, but wariness persisted.

''What would you folks like to do this afternoon?'' Tom asked as the meal came to an end. ''I'm afraid I've neglected my duties as a host. Kath says I'm hopeless when I get down here at the lake—all I can think about is fishing. Marilee?'' He turned to the woman on his right. ''I know you're not much of a fisherman—maybe you'd like to take a spin around the lake later on this afternoon. There're some mighty pretty places I could show you.''

Propping her elbows on the table to rest her chin provocatively in her hands, Marilee smiled up at her host through a sweep of sooty lashes. ''Tom, you and Kathy are incredible. If any other man had said that to me, especially in the presence of his own wife, I'd wonder, but with you two...'' She shook her head, then turned a mischievous look on Marsh. ''Do you know what I'd really like to do? I'd love to drive into Charleston for dinner and dancing tonight. Tom? Kathy? How about it—Kath really needs a break from all this heavy cooking, and I know I could stand a little dose of civilization. Too much of this lovely peace and quiet of yours, and I'm afraid I'll go native.''

The woman was incredible! Persia bit her tongue on a sharp rebuke, silently willing Chip to open fire. Maybe she was being hypersensitive, but if she had to listen to much more of Marilee's brand of patronization, she'd spade up the whole backyard.

Ancient memories prompted a gleam of amusement in her dark eyes as she sloshed her half-melted ice around in her glass. How many times had she come home from school, furious and hurting from some spiteful remark, and spaded up row after row of her father's precious Velvet Bent grass? Lucy, bless her, had understood, and had protected her from Hans's and her father's wrath. Hans had finally given up on trying to patch the ruined turf, and by the time she'd left for college, half the backyard had been turned into an impromptu flower garden.

"How about it, Persia? Care for a moratorium on our wager? We could pick up where we left off tomorrow if you'd like to take a break from your diet tonight."

Marilee squirmed delicately. "Oh—but I thought..."

Persia knew very well what she'd thought. It was extremely tempting, but reluctantly, she passed up the chance to spoil Marilee's romantic evening. She was growing to dislike the woman more with every passing day, but if Marilee was Marsh's choice, then there was little point in creating friction. Besides, she couldn't do that to Tom and Kathy. Bless them, they were both so naive that Marilee's little putdowns passed completely over their heads.

Why couldn't Marsh see beyond all that laquered perfection and the sugar-coated mannerisms? "Thanks for the invitation, Marsh," she said evenly, "but I'd rather stay here.'' Then, her mobile mouth twitching in a teasing grin, she added, ''Relax, you can trust me not to cheat. Chip can throw his body across the refrigerator door and guard it until you get back.''

It was settled with little more discussion. Kathy insisted that she really enjoyed the chance to cook—''I'm so tied up with committee work at home that half the time I rush in five minutes before Tom gets home and throw something together—but I *never* turn down a chance to go dancing.''

Marilee leaned back in her chair, her eyes gleaming with pale green satisfaction. Chip said nothing, but Persia felt safe in counting on his cooperation. It was odd how quickly a feeling of guarded camaraderie had sprung up between the two of them, in spite of the misery he'd caused her in the past. She'd far rather suffer through an evening of Chip's disconcerting silences and acid observations than spend the evening watching Marilee and Marsh draped around each other's necks on a dance floor. She really would lose her appetite if she had to sit through that—either that or she'd devour everything in sight.

Persia stood up and gathered her dishes. ''Well, now that everyone's got over the initial shock of seeing me in my bathing suit,'' she announced breezily, ''I think I'll go out on the pier and bake my bones for a while.'' She rinsed her plate and glass and turned them down in the dishwasher. ''If you'll put away the perishables, Kath, I'll take care of the rest when I come in again.''

Her glance snagged on Marsh's frown. Puzzled, she paused on her way out. ''What's wrong? Don't you trust me in the kitchen alone?''

''I told you last night,'' he said in a low, grim voice, ''don't put yourself down.''

''But I—''

''You're not even aware of it, are you? You're so used

to making a big joke out of everything, you do it unconsciously.''

"Marsh, you're being ridiculous. When did I ever put myself down?'' Before he could answer, she went on with growing indignation. "And furthermore, what business is it of yours?''

He continued to study her with a look of inbred arrogance, and then he shrugged. "You're perfectly right. It's none of my business if you want to feel sorry for yourself. I—''

"*Sorry* for myself!'' she squawked. "Spare me the pop psychology, will you? Save it for your faithful readers! I don't need you to tell me what to think—about myself or anything else!''

"Oh, Lord, are you two at it again?'' Kathy groaned, grabbing their two arms and dragging them bodily into the next room.

Persia's eyes sparkled indignantly at Marsh's unjust accusation. Sorry for herself? She abhorred self-pity! Size or no size, she prided herself on being totally healthy, both physically and mentally. Barring a slight tendency toward daydreams, of course.

"What *is* it with you people?'' Kathy persisted. "Marsh, haven't you forgiven her yet for what she did to you at our reception? And you, Persia—you ought to be ashamed! Just because you had a silly schoolgirl crush on Marsh all those years ago and he forgot to dance with you, that's no reason to keep picking fights with him now.''

As wave after wave of anguished embarrassment flowed over her, Persia felt her face grow hot. *How could you, Kathy?* she wailed silently. With regal dignity, she turned and walked carefully to the foot of the stairs. She could have balanced a stack of encyclopedias on her head and not lost a single volume as she climbed gracefully to the sanctuary of her room.

Totally without guile, Kathy could have no idea of how mortifying her disclosure had been. Persia shook her head in helpless disbelief as she went through the motions of getting out of her clothes. And then she stood there for several minutes, staring distractedly at the heap of clothing, wondering why she'd undressed in the middle of the day.

"Snap out of it," she muttered. "You were going to sunbathe." Woodenly, she stepped into her bathing suit and tugged the straps up over her arms. There was only one way to handle an impossible situation like this. Hiding in her room for two weeks was impractical; she'd simply have to brazen it out, pretend it didn't exist—pretend she had met Marsh for the first time a few days ago.

How little it took to crack the veneer she'd polished so assiduously these past ten years. For a moment she'd been sixteen all over again—sixteen, fat, painfully self-conscious, and experiencing the first bewildering stirring of grown-up passion.

After braiding her hair in one thick pigtail and locating her beach towel, she marched downstairs, head high, eyes front and center. There was no one in evidence but Chip.

"Going swimming, I see."

Persia shot him a suspicious glance. Stating the obvious was not normally one of Chip's failings. "Sunbathing," she corrected.

"Why?"

That was more like it. If he didn't care to launch a frontal attack, he'd throw you off balance with an irrelevant question.

"Because I think I look marvellous with cherry-red cheeks, a beet-red nose, and a lobster-red back, okay?"

"Does everything remind you of food?"

With an exasperated sigh, she dropped her towel and sat

down on the edge of the sofa. "No. As a matter of fact, Cracker Jacks make me think of tin whistles."

"Persia, am I attractive to you—as a man, I mean?"

It was several moments before Persia realized that her jaw was hanging. She snapped it shut, swallowed, and tried to think of a tactful way of answering the question.

"Don't bother," Chip said witheringly. "That's why she left me, you know. I'm a nerd. No woman is turned on by a skinny guy with thick glasses and thin hair."

Persia resisted the impulse to pull him onto her lap and comfort him. "What about Woody Allen? Have you noticed the sort of women he attracts?"

"The guitar player? I thought he was dead." Chip sighed despondently.

"That's Woodier Guthrie. Look, lots of men wear glasses. Marsh does," she reasoned.

"Yeah, and Marsh has hair and the sort of body that appeals to a woman. He's got every woman here panting after him—except maybe Kathy."

Persia chose to ignore that particular observation. "Look, Chip, you're being oversensitive," she insisted. "I know Ann. If she didn't love you, she'd never have married you. You can believe it."

"So if she loves me so much, how come she left me?" he shot back with irrefutable logic.

"Oh—! Look, go change into your trunks and come out on the pier with me. We'll discuss it out there."

"Oh, sure, and you can lust after my manly torso," Chip sneered.

"Stop being so down on yourself and come on! You'd look terrific with a tan, you know—your hair would get all streaky blond, and your eyes would look stunning."

Hands shoved deeply into the pockets of his brown trousers, Chip looked at her anxiously. "You're sure you don't mind company? I'm rotten at small talk."

She laughed openly at that. "So I'd noticed. Teach me all you know about computers and I'll give you lessons in small talk. Fair enough?"

"Fair enough."

But once out on the pier, they never got around to discussing computers, nor did Chip need any encouragement to pour out his insecurities. Persia made him use a sunscreen, and then he stretched out beside her, his royal-blue trunks billowing stiffly about his hips. He proceeded to give her a painfully detailed account of his marital problems.

She listened silently, her attention wandering only occasionally as she wondered what the others were doing. Before too long, Marilee would be monopolizing the bathroom while she got herself ready for tonight's date.

"Why did you let her go?"

"Let her! What was I supposed to do when she told me she'd been bored stiff since the second day of our honeymoon?"

That one took some consideration. Brainy he may be; Chip was *not* among the world's most fascinating men. He'd been odd man out all his life, just as she had been. He spoke an entirely different language from his classmates, and when they'd grown tired of trying to communicate with him, they'd turned to ignoring him. He'd retaliated by cultivating a streak of defensive maliciousness, and that had only made matters worse. Persia herself had avoided him like the plague whenever she could—what girl likes to be told that one of her thighs is being considered for the site of a new state park?

"Have you seriously tried to do something about it?"

"I wouldn't know where to start," he said hopelessly. He was beginning to toast, even with the moderate sunscreen he'd applied. Persia rolled off her towel and tossed it to him.

"Here, cover up. You can't get it all in one sitting."

"You should know. I remember how you looked at the wedding. Every car within three blocks came to a complete stop and waited for you to turn green."

"Now *that's* small talk. In fact, it's downright petty." Oddly enough, it didn't hurt, though. She knew he hadn't meant it.

Chip sighed and reached for the sunscreen, uncapping it and dousing his face again. Without his glasses he looked as helpless as a three-day-old chick.

"Chip, have you ever thought about getting contacts? Here—how about rubbing some more of that stuff on my back?" She sidled around so that he could reach her, and her gaze wandered up toward the house and lingered there. While Chip spread the scented lotion over her shoulders with nervous, jerky strokes, she wondered where Marsh was and what he was doing. What had he meant by that crack about putting herself down, anyway? And why had it angered him so?

"I thought about it. So I'd be a nerd with contacts. Terrific."

"Stop it! You're *not* a nerd! You're a very—you're an extremely—well, you can *change*, can't you? Look at what happened to me? Do you know that I didn't even have my first kiss until I was almost twenty years old?"

He smiled weakly. "I was twenty-four. I've never even kissed any woman but Ann." His voice took on a doleful tone. "I don't guess I'll ever kiss any woman again."

"Oh, ye gods, spare me the pathos! You want to know what it's like? I'll show you what it's like! Come here!"

A few minutes later they strolled slowly up to the house, heads together as Persia earnestly entreated him to give Ann a call. "Tell her *I* want to see her. Tell her you want to take her out for dinner and dancing. Tell her anything, but get her here."

"I can't dance."

"Who cares! You can learn, can't you?"

"Would you——?"

"Only if you call her," Persia specified. At this rate, her vacation was going to be spent shoring up Chip's confidence. She'd given him a lesson in kissing—the last thing in the world she'd ever expected to have to do—and she'd promised to take him to a hair stylist and a decent men's shop in Charleston and give him a new image. Ann could thank her later.

Marsh waited on the screened porch until they headed up toward the house. His temper had risen steadily until it was pounding at his temples. It had reached flash point when he'd watched her kiss that poor bastard to within an inch of his life. He'd been admiring her so damned much for her refreshing wholesomeness, and all the time, underneath all that sunny, innocent exterior, she was totally unprincipled. Wasn't Ann Gaillard supposed to be a friend of hers? Friends didn't wait for a sign of weakness and then strike where they could do the most damage!

Angrily stubbing out his cigar, he stood and waited for them. Dammit, it was hitting below the belt! When Marilee had broken off their relationship and then married Kurtz within a month, he'd felt like going up to Chicago and raiding that damned gold-plated hotel and bringing her back across his shoulder. Instead, he'd burned out his rage on work and on the racquetball court. Even when he'd heard rumors of their marriage being on the skids, he'd purposely stayed clear.

It had been Marilee who'd made the first move. And because the divorce had been one of those so-called friendly ones, with the two of them still as cozy as Sears and Roebuck, he'd held back on making any definite move. Only now, after her divorce had been final for just over a year, had he taken the first step to put their relationship on a more official basis. Pretty damned commendable, if he did say so himself. Hadn't he been crazy about the woman for years? Besides, it was time he got married, and one way or another, he'd already invested so many years on her, he didn't really know any other suitable candidates.

With lowering brows, Marsh watched the pair of them swinging up the boardwalk that extended from the pier to the circular driveway. Those long, lush legs of hers made that poor devil look anemic. No wonder he was gazing up at her as if she were some sort of goddess.

Well, he'd set her straight, all right. He might be considered old-fashioned, but there were some things that just weren't done. Moving out of the shade of the porch, he strode down to meet them, his purposeful stride making no sound on the mossy old bricks that paved the way from the house to the drive.

"Persia! *There* you are."

It was Tom. He'd come around the house before Marsh got halfway down the walk. Frustrated, Marsh watched as she dismissed Chip with a sickening little pat on the hand and beamed her seductive smile on her own cousin's husband.

Marsh wheeled away with a muffled oath and strode back to the house. It was a good thing he was going out tonight. He couldn't trust himself to be civil to her. Damn all predatory females who raided other people's marriages as if they were bargain counters! Now he knew why she'd been so eager to stay home with that scrawny little weasel.

A mental image of Persia's lush, honey-colored flesh juxtaposed with Chip's pale white carcass made him head for the medicine chest. With ill concealed impatience, he wrestled the childproof cap off a bottle of antacid tablets.

"She's never said much about it, but I happen to know she's been wanting one for years—I just kept putting it off," Tom murmured. "There was always something—the car, the air conditioner, my new office furniture. And then we found out we had termites."

"She'll love it, Tom!" exclaimed Persia. "I wish I could see her face when she walks in and finds it there. Is it a baby or a concert grand? You're going to have to load it up and move it in a few months, remember?"

"I know, it was crazy to get the thing now, but with our anniversary and all, I just decided to go ahead and shoot the works. She's so good—she deserves more than I'll ever be able to give her."

Persia felt a twist of something sharp inside her. Tom was one in a million, and if anyone deserved him, Kathy did. They were two of the nicest people she knew—even if Kathy was occasionally a little too candid for comfort. She hugged him impulsively. "Dibs on you the next time around."

By the time Persia had showered and dressed, it was almost five-thirty. There'd been a run on the bathrooms, with four of them getting dressed to go out. After coming inside, she'd curled up on her bed with a mystery, but she'd been far too preoccupied to read. The effects of Kathy's tactless disclosure had already faded—it had been an innocent blunder, and Persia had never been one to nurse grievances. But there was still Chip's problem to consider, not to mention the delightful surprise Tom had in store for his wife. Kathy had studied piano for ten years, and was still playing the old studio upright she'd started on. Persia would have gladly given her the baby grand she'd agonized over for three years, but it had long since been sold.

Her mood began to take a nosedive as soon as she left her room to go downstairs. Marilee and Kathy were somewhere down the hall chattering about where they were going tonight, and Tom's plaintive baritone overrode Marilee's well-modulated drawl with a mild complaint about having to button up and put on a necktie.

Persia's hand moved slowly over the cool satin wood of the bannister. Sometimes it seemed as if the whole world was made up of pairs. Even Chip was half of a pair. He and Ann would get back together again, if she had to handcuff them and make them listen to reason.

As for herself, there were times when she felt like a single bookend. She'd prided herself on the way she'd handled the termination of her engagement just three months before the wedding was to have taken place. At the expense of one broken spade handle and her carefully nurtured fingernails, she'd dealt with the emotional trauma of being told that she just wasn't the sort of wife a future gubernatorial candidate needed. That had been Mrs. Blake. Patrick had worded it a bit more diplomatically when he'd come to see her following his mother's little visit. He'd stammered something about divergent interests and taking more time to be really, *really* certain.

She'd seen through his embarrassed little speech. He'd loved her a little, but he loved his mother's money and the power it could wield a lot more. Persia had given him back his ring—it had been far too ostentatious for her tastes, anyway; hardly the thing to wear with gardening clothes. Graciously, she'd told him that she'd been wanting to break the engagement for weeks.

"We'll be much better friends this way," she'd told him. And then she'd gone about the business of patching up her poor battered pride. Once more she'd dragged out her favorite fantasy and buried herself in its illusory comfort.

"You're really something, do you know that?" Marsh said softly as she reached the bottom of the stairs.

"Oh—you startled me! Well, thanks," she added doubtfully. His deep-set eyes seemed to hold an admiring gleam, but his tone was decidedly cool.

Persia felt her spirits bottom out and begin to climb again. He was dressed in a flawlessly tailored summer-weight suit, and his face had that freshly shaven look that made her want to touch it. The contrast between his formidible jawline and the newly softened skin over it was irresistable.

"Oh, it's no compliment," he told her, his eyes moving disdainfully over the cool cotton dress that skimmed her breasts and fell gracefully to the tops of her bare feet. "I hope you can resurrect enough common decency to behave yourself tonight. Just remember, we won't be gone for long, and once I get back, I'll be watching you like a hawk. Think about it," he finished with chilling intensity.

He turned to leave, and Persia called after him. "Marsh! You come back here! What's got into you, anyway? You started the whole thing, and now you're jumping on *me?*"

He turned, his narrowed gaze scouring her face unmercifully. "Don't blame your shortcomings on me, Persia. It's past time you grew up and learned that you can't have everything you want just because you happen to want it."

"My shortcomings?" she marveled, wondering what had happened that could turn a playful wager into a vendetta. Good Lord, it wasn't all that important. What difference did a few pounds make?

"You had me fooled, I'll admit," he jeered. "You don't know the meaning of the word integrity. Well, just remember what I said—you either behave yourself, or I'll make you sorry you ever showed up for this house party." He stalked off, not trusting himself to say more. Damn her, she had no business prancing around here like a snub-nosed little houri, setting her trap for every man in sight! Tom and Kathy had one of the best marriages going, but no relationship was immune to deliberate sabotage by a woman like Persia.

It occurred to him to wonder why he was reacting so strongly. His steps slowed as he considered the facts. Fact one: A woman who was nothing more to him than a friend had been a little too affectionate with a couple of married men. Was he afraid Tom wouldn't know how to handle it?

Hell, Tom was a big boy now. When it came to women, Tom had a much better track record than he did. At least Tom hadn't stood by and let another man walk off with the woman he was practically engaged to, and then calmly taken her back again when she'd come running back home.

Maybe that was part of the problem, Marsh admitted. Ever since Kurtz had stolen Marilee right out from under his nose, raiders—of either sex—had struck a nerve in him. And Persia was the last woman he'd have suspected of playing around with another woman's man. Maybe that refreshing artlessness of hers had blinded them all to her true nature. If she made up her mind to play around, what man could resist her?

Chip was a pushover—he'd be full of self-doubts and ripe for some sweet-talking female, and Tom wouldn't be the first man to get restless after the novelty had worn off his marriage.

Why didn't she turn her sights on fair game? Was she one of those women who hunted strictly for the sake of sport, taking special pleasure in poaching on someone else's territory? If she thought for one minute he was going to stand idly by and watch while she took potshots at everything in pants, she was sadly mistaken. He'd sacrifice his own personal happiness before he let her do that. He owed Tom that much, at least.

He was beginning to see now why she didn't have much to say about this Blake fellow; a bird in the hand was no challenge. Maybe he ought to do everybody a favor and put in a call to Virginia. On the other hand, why not give himself the satisfaction of personally putting her out of action?

Ignoring his deepest instincts, Marsh goaded himself into a fine state of self-righteousness, rationalizing a task he was beginning to savor intensely. So she'd had a crush on him ten years ago, had she? And she thought she could blame her roving eye and her voracious appetite for conquest on a schoolgirl disappointment? Great. He enjoyed a challenge—and he had nothing better to do over the next week and a half. We'd see how she liked it when the tables were turned.

Chapter Five

As the last rays of daylight left the sky, Persia curled up against one of the pilings on the end of the pier, absently listening to drifts of soft music, snatches of distant laughter, and the buzz of a quiet trolling motor. Now and then a fish jumped. The scent of backyard barbecues hung low in the air to mingle with the sweetness of magnolia and sapindus saponaria—her old favorite chinaberry.

A half-forgotten memory emerged from her dreamy contemplation. One of her favorite things as a child had been helping Lucy clean and puncture the small round seeds, and then dyeing and stringing them into necklaces. Lucy's sister had had several chinaberry trees in her clean-swept yard, but to Persia's disappointment, Hans had adamantly refused to adulterate the effect of his regal evergreens, magnolias and Japanese weeping cherrys with a single lowly chinaberry.

A light came on in the kitchen, and reluctantly she unfolded herself to wander slowly back up to the house. This would probably be as good a time as any to start working on Chip. The haircut and the new clothes could wait—the important thing was for him to make contact. The longer he waited, the more difficult it would be.

He was seated at the table, staring morosely at the last wedge of the Lady Baltimore cake. "I thought it might help," he said despondently. "Want to split it?"

Persia experienced a small surge of revulsion. "No, thanks. I'm not hungry."

"Afraid of what Marsh will say?" Chip taunted, shoving the cake away as if he, too, had lost his appetite.

"Certainly not! If I wanted it, I'd eat it. Besides," she added wistfully, "the bet's probably off now. Marsh got upset about something and started throwing his weight around, and..." The words trailed off as she stared dejectedly at the scalloped rim of the cake plate.

Absently, Chip reached for a crumb that had fallen to the tablecover. "What set him off? That red-haired piranha of his finally getting to him?"

Persia collected a streak of frosting on her finger and nibbled at it thoughtfully. "You mean Marilee? Don't let Kathy hear you call her that. They've been best buddies since the seventh grade, and no mere brother-in-law is going to come between them now."

Breaking off half the top layer, Chip glared across the table indignantly. "Yeah, well if Marilee had had her way, I wouldn't even *be* Kath's brother-in-law. She made a play for Tom two weeks before the wedding."

"You're kidding!" Orderly by nature, Persia evened off the jagged edge of the cake. "Then what are they doing inviting her here now? In fact, why did Kathy have her for a maid of honor?"

"She never knew. Tom couldn't tell her—not that she'd have believed him, anyway. Kath had gone to Atlanta shopping that weekend, and Marilee got Tom to show her the apartment they'd rented. I happened to be there wiring in Tom's speakers, and I heard her. She was telling him all about how far he could go with her help—her grandfather was old Judge MacKay, you know.'' Chip snorted in disgust. ''She was running her fingers up his lapels and giving him the eye—no telling how far she'd have gone if I hadn't dropped my cutting pliers.''

Persia stared unseeingly at a figgy lump in the frosting. ''I wouldn't have thought Tom was her style. I heard her telling Kathy once when they were in senior high that she'd never date a man who had to live on his capital. I thought she was talking about the White House—I had visions of her turning up her nose at John F.''

''Yeah, well if she thinks Marsh is rolling in it, she hasn't done her homework. I don't know what happened, but when old Moss Randolph split for France with his new family, the big bucks split with him. It's either in France or in a Swiss bank, but it sure as shooting isn't in South Carolina anymore. Ann's old man is president of the bank, remember? And even in binary, certain things add up.''

Persia's forefinger sought out a large crumb and captured it. ''So what's the difference? She's always been in love with him, according to Kath.''

''Look, Persia,'' Chip said earnestly, ''next to Ann, I love Kathy better than anybody in the world, but let's face it—she's a babe in the woods. Everybody's always protected her because she's little.''

''Not to mention disgustingly nice. I used to envy her so much I could taste it.'' Persia scooped up a fingerfull of filling and thoughtfully licked it off. ''At least Tom's safe now. Marilee's got her sights set on another target.''

''Yeah,'' Chip agreed somberly, lifting the remaining slab of cake to scrape up the soft moist part that stuck to the plate. "Rough on you, but I guess people like us are—"

"Rough on me! What do you mean, rough on me?" Persia pierced the barrier of Chip's thick lenses with an indignant glare.

"Oh, come on, Persia, knock it off," he said derisively. "Who do you think you're kidding?"

Indignation crumbled and fell away, leaving her totally defenseless. She made a valiant effort to refute the accusation, but it was no good. "I'm not...am I that transparent?"

Shrugging his bony shoulders, Chip said candidly, "To me you are, but I doubt if anyone else has noticed. If it would help, I'd tell you he wasn't worth it, but we both know that's a lie."

Sympathy from such a totally unexpected source was almost her undoing. Blinking rapidly, she said in a thickening voice, "Oh, well—back to the drawing board. Next time I'll pick out a man with better taste—someone who prefers a woman with an earthy bent and a little meat on her bones."

"Speaking of which," Chip said dryly, "you may as well finish off that last bite. No point in leaving a dirty plate."

Persia's brow puckered into a frown. "What happened to the cake?"

"You ate it."

"Oh, no! Honestly, I don't even remember it."

"Then it won't show up on the scales. Trust me—I know my physics."

After washing the plate, drying it and putting it away, Persia glanced at the clock. Only nine-twenty—a whole miserable evening to get through, and as if she didn't have enough to worry about, she had to go and pull a stunt like that. It would have been nice to have *some*thing going for her—like the ability to stick to a diet for three consecutive days.

Entering the living room, she stopped short. Chip was standing stiffly in front of the fern-filled fireplace, his rumpled figure registering steely determination. He scowled at her fiercely. "Could you lend me five dollars?"

"Well—sure. Right now?"

"Right now," he said forcefully. His prematurely thinning hair was standing on end, and one side of his collar was poking up. Behind the thick glasses, his eyes burned with newfound resolution. "I'm going after her."

"Ann?" Persia hazarded.

"Who did you think? Who've we been talking about all night?"

"Me. And Marsh—and Kathy, and Marilee and Tom," she listed wonderingly. Could he have had a drink while she'd been finishing up in the kitchen?

He shot her a withering look, uncomfortably reminiscent of the ones she'd been subjected to back when they'd been children. "She's in Orangeburg at her sister's. If I called her she wouldn't talk to me. I'm going to get her and bring her here, and you can talk some sense into her. Like you did me."

"I did?" Persia marveled. True—she'd had plans of that sort, but she'd scarcely had time to put them into action. Still, she agreed with him—the important thing now was to get them talking to each other again. And if they were here, she'd be on hand to do a little discreet meddling if the occasion called for it.

"Let me get my purse," she said, hurrying for the stairs. "Will five be enough?"

"Yeah—I just need some gas money. I forgot to go to the bank before I left home."

Oh, Lord, could he even find his way there in the dark? Could he read a road map? Persia smothered her misgivings and saw him off. The Gaillards' *enfant terrible* was twenty-seven now. If he wasn't responsible at his age, then nothing she could do at this point would help. He needed Ann. Together, they made a perfect unit. Ann's quiet, sweet practicality would compensate for Chip's acute introversion.

Surprisingly, Persia found herself liking him more all the time. It was easy in retrospect to see what had happened; he'd grown so accustomed to the cycle of misunderstanding, mistrust, rejection and attack, that at the first sign of trouble, he barricaded himself and started fighting back. After so many years, he didn't even wait for the first shot to be fired.

Turning away from the door after watching the taillights disappear around the curve, Persia was struck by a single unpalatable aspect of the coming reunion. If Ann came back here with Chip, things were going to be a little awkward. Three cozy couples and a spare. Could she take it? On the other hand, did she have any choice? If she left now, it would be pretty obvious. Between Chip's perspicacity and Kathy's innocent tactlessness—not to mention Marilee's double-edged tongue—the few shreds of pride she had left would be sliced to ribbons and hung out to dry.

She'd been asleep for some time when she heard the others arriving. Her window looked down on the front yard, and sounds carried quite clearly on the still night air.

On her stomach, she pulled the pillow over her head and attempted to close her mind to the muffled sounds of sleepy conversation and weary footsteps. Three sets of footsteps. One—Marilee's—turned right at the top of the stairs, and the others, Tom's and Kathy's, trailed off in the opposite direction.

Had they left Marsh somewhere along the way? Unless

he'd mellowed considerably, she couldn't much blame them. Persia lifted the pillow from her head and tossed it on the floor. Flopping over on her back, she tugged impatiently at her twisted nightgown. What had they done with him? Could he and Marilee have had a squabble?

An irreverent surge of glee shot through her; dutifully, she tried to subdue it. It was bad, bad, *bad* to harbor any such hopes. All the same, considering Marsh's disposition when they'd left here, there was no telling what might have happened. He'd been in a foul mood for some reason. That peculiar little episode at the foot of the stairs, for instance. If he'd handled Marilee with the same degree of finesse, then they probably weren't even speaking by now.

Persia sighed despondently. Even if they weren't, Marsh would soon come to his senses. And when he did, three guesses which fence he'd start mending first.

A slight sound caused her to glance up. The door at the foot of her narrow old spool bed opened a crack, and she squinted blearily at the light from the hallway. A tall, shadowy figure appeared, hovering in the opening, and she blinked her eyes open. "Tom? Is that you? What's wrong?"

The door opened wider. Even before it had closed again, leaving the room in silvery darkness, she knew it wasn't Tom.

"Where is he?" came Marsh's terse whisper.

"Where's who—Tom?" she whispered back, sitting up and pulling the sheet up to her chin.

"Don't play games with me, Persia. He's not in his room. I thought he'd be with you."

"In bed?" she crowed disbelievingly. Then, lowering her voice again, she said, "If you're looking for Chip, he's gone to Orangeburg. He probably won't be back until tomorrow—and maybe not even then. It depends on what happens when he gets there." One small segment of her mind was concerned with answering a question; the rest of it was marveling at how the mere presence of another human being could alter the atmosphere in a room.

The hard mattress gave under Marsh's weight as he sat down beside her, and she reeled from the potent spell of his nearness—the hint of aftershave, the faint smell of bourbon, the warm, clean scent of his body.

"What are you up to now, Persia? What happened while you two were here alone together?"

His rough whisper was incredibly intimate, and it took several moments before the meaning of his words struck home. Persia's thoughts flew immediately to the cake she'd demolished without even realizing it. They swerved back to the intimidating figure that was crowding her up against the wall, and indignation struggled with guilt. Both emotions were almost lost under a tide of rising excitement that shimmered in the air between them.

For safety's sake, she hung on to the indignation. "I don't know just when you decided to set yourself up as my keeper, Marsh, but believe me, I don't need any tinhorn tyrant telling me—"

"Ah *ha!*" Large, hard hands bit into her soft upper arms, and he pulled her around so that she was facing him in the tense darkness. His voice was like torn velvet. "The best defense is an offense, huh? I can smell guilt a mile away! If you weren't trying to hide something, you wouldn't be—"

She wrestled herself away, rubbing her arms where his fingers had sunk into her flesh. "Guilt? You're damn right, I'm guilty! So sue me! I'm sick and tired of your silly old bet, anyhow!" Her voice had risen to a shrill whisper, and he grabbed her again, covering her mouth with the hard palm of his hand.

"What do you mean, my bet? The diet thing?" he

growled, moving his mouth to within inches of her ear. "What does any of this have to do with a damned diet?"

Her mouth was still covered, and the muffled sounds she was able to make were unintelligible, so she bit him. In the process of sinking her teeth into the fleshy mound at the base of his thumb, her tongue flicked across his palm. She felt the quick hardening of his anger just before he yelped.

Both of them froze instinctively. Persia waited for the door to be thrown open. She braced herself to explain an exceedingly embarrassing situation. When nothing happened, she resumed her silent struggle against Marsh's overpowering strength. A warm current of bourbon scented breath caressed her cheek as she managed to wrench her head free. He could have no idea what he was doing to her, how the feel of his hands on her naked skin weakened her powers of resistance.

Heaven help her, she didn't want to resist. "Let me go, Marsh! You're drunk!" Her heart was leaping around in her breast like a wild thing—and his was little better. Wasn't he even aware of the dangers of what they were doing?

"You bit me," he accused. "You took a chunk out of my hand!"

She succeeded in freeing one arm, only to have it tucked behind her as Marsh shoved her down on the bed. "So I got a few more calories of protein," she panted. "I'll make up for it at breakfast." This wasn't the way her fantasy was supposed to go! Daydreams had never caused this shuddering, driving need inside her.

"Persia." The soft rasp of his voice saying her name merged with her imagination. Before she could direct her mind and body back on a sane course, it came again. "Persia?" he whispered tentatively, tenderly, and then he kissed her.

No child's kiss, this. No butterfly wings—no velvet touch. At the heady taste of him, Persia melted in his arms, lost to reason, lost to all thought of anything that wasn't Marsh. Her free arm came around his neck, and when he loosened his hold to slide his arms around her, she wrapped her other arm around his waist.

Molten lava streamed down shuddering hills, into hidden valleys, igniting every nerve in her body. The sweet musky taste of his mouth drove her wild. The feel of his hands as they stroked her naked shoulders was incredibly arousing. Her toes curled slowly, and she began to writhe as a hot liquid urgency filled her body. When she felt one thin strap of her gown give way, she knew an irrational urge to tear the other one free. She wanted to feel the sensuous textures of his body against her naked skin, chest against breast, thigh against thigh.

His mouth settled softly on her eyelids, her nose, her chin. His lips explored the shallow dimple in her left cheek and then moved on to her ear, and her movements beneath him grew more restless. She whispered his name as a protest, only to have it emerge as a litany of incoherent sounds.

"Hush, my sweet—hush, now," he rasped softly against her temple. Sliding the thin skirt of her gown up, he let his hand close gently over her thigh.

Careful, warned a part of him that stood aloof to gaze down reprovingly. The drinks he'd downed during the past five unending hours had done little to enhance his judgment.

But his eager senses were beyond the reach of reason, heightened by a brooding anger that had been growing in him all evening, by an unreasonable jealousy that had sprung up from nowhere. Inflamed by the touch, the taste, the scent of her, he summarily dismissed his own warning.

His hand moved higher, settling on the gentle curve of

her stomach. He could feel the tremors going through her, hear the soft catch of her breath. So rich, so warm, so womanly...he ached with the wanting of her!

He felt her fingers moving up and down the hollow of his spine—when had she managed to loosen his shirt? Gasping, he curled his fingers convulsively into her satiny flesh as she touched a particularly sensitive spot.

"Easy, sweet—take it easy," he groaned. Oh Lord, this wasn't at all smart—this had been the farthest thing from his mind when he'd opened that door, and now he was almost past the point of no return. He lifted his head from the enticing curve of her throat, struggling to resist the heady temptation of her lips. She was incredibly sweet— the clean flower scent of her skin, the silken texture of her hair...

This was irrational. His mind reached out desperately for an anchor, for some fragment of reality that could stem this irresistible tide. *Think, man! Think of what you're doing! This is Persia—this is not some woman you can sate yourself with tonight and then walk away from in the morning.*

It was no use. His head fell softly against her breast and slipped down into the scented valley. A firm, impudent button nudged his cheek. He turned his face and took it into his mouth, and he was lost again. Her response was instantaneous. There was no holding back, no false pretense of reluctance. She was all woman, and for now, she was his.

He shifted, securing a position between her thighs— damn it, he had on too many clothes and he couldn't stop loving her long enough to remove them. You'd think that at his age he'd know how it was done.

Her hands were urging him away, tugging at his shirt. Oh, sweet heaven, she was as eager as he was.

"Marsh," she panted hoarsely, twisting sensuously as he pressed his fiercely aroused body into hers.

"Don't talk, precious—please," he groaned. Aching with the heaviness of desire, he didn't dare risk the chance of coming to his senses. Not now—not until he'd extinguished this wild, raging inferno she'd lighted in his body.

His tongue caressed the small, baroque crown of one breast as his hands explored the rich intricacies of her body. How could anyone so wonderful to look at, to touch, to taste, be so—? A tiny corner of his brain reminded him that he was furious with her. The way she'd come on to Chip, the way she'd beamed that thousand-watt smile at Tom—he'd vowed to teach her a lesson, but this wasn't the lesson he'd had in mind. Somewhere along the way he'd taken a wrong turn.

"Please, Marsh."

He closed his eyes against the sliver of reason that threatened to encroach on his warm, tantalizing paradise. Desperately, he tried to tear his thoughts away, to regain some vestige of control over the situation. *I'm thirty-six years old, damn it! No clever, sleepy-eyed seductress is going to put one over on me!*

He felt the strong surge of her hips beneath him as she responded to his fevered caresses, writhing and twisting until he was pushed to the far edge of sanity. "Easy, love, just let me get rid of some clothes," he rasped hotly.

"Marsh, dammit!" She twisted aside and braced herself up on one elbow. "My foot's caught and I can't move it."

As swiftly and as unexpectedly as it had arisen, the sexual excitement ebbed, leaving him feeling drained and slightly ludicrous. He rolled away and sat on the edge of the bed, holding his head in his hands.

"Marsh," Persia whispered plaintively, "I can't get my foot out. It's wedged between the spokes of the bed."

* * *

"Now, they'll be here anytime, so I think we should all clear out and give them some space." Kathy stood, fists bracing her thirty-three-inch hips, and rapped out orders like a miniature general. "Marilee, if you want to get your hair done, I can drive you in, or you can take my car. Tom and Marsh will go fishing again, and Persia—would you rather go to town with us, or go fishing with the men?"

Given her choice, Persia would rather have sunk to the bottom of the deepest part of Lake Moultrie. Short of that, she'd rather stay clear of the whole shooting match. "Why don't I stay home and tackle the backyard while you all do your things? If Ann and Chip come, I promise I'll duck down behind the bushes."

Persia and Marilee were seated at the table. Marilee nibbled on her breakfast of dry cereal and strawberries, and Persia stared miserably at her own bowl of fruit. She'd purposely waited until she'd heard the men go out fishing before coming downstairs, uneager to face Marsh after last night's debacle.

Which one of them would feel more foolish in the clear light of day? He'd been in his cups, and her common sense had been short-circuited by a persistent fantasy. He'd spouted some nonsense about her being guilty, and then he'd pounced.

How did he know she was guilty? Had he weighed and measured every bite of forbidden food in the kitchen before he'd left, and again when he'd got home? But that was ridiculous! No sane man took someone else's diet all that seriously. She didn't herself, now that she'd trimmed down to the pleasingly plump category. Except for sporadic efforts aimed at fitting into a certain outfit, that is— or foolish attempts to impress a certain person.

Good Lord, Cleopatra had had a double chin—Venus de Milo was certainly no rack of bones! Look at Sophie Tucker—look at Mae West. Did they ruin their lives over a few surplus pounds, a little excess padding here and there?

Marsh could pack up his petty dictator act and go take a flying leap. She refused to have the rest of her vacation ruined by his hot and cold running disposition. It was enough to ruin any woman's appetite, diet or no diet. Fantasy or no fantasy.

"Aren't you going to eat your berries?" Kathy inquired solicitously. "Do you want a little cream and sugar on them?"

A grim smile lighted Persia's eyes as she reached for the sugar bowl, but before she'd had time to do more then anticipate, Tom and Marsh strolled in, grinning broadly and smelling of fish.

"You know that lunker I've been trying to catch for two and a half years? Do you know what he fell for? Red worms. A stinking little bundle of red worms on a bream hook! After all the tackle I've snagged, and all the shiners I've sacrificed, I watched this son of a gun here land him on three pound test and a mess of worms." Tom shook his head and turned to the sink.

"Use the lavatory, Tom—don't wipe fish scales all over my clean sink."

"Yes ma'am," Tom replied with playful meekness. "What are you ladies up to now? Plotting another night on the town? Persia, honey, you didn't miss much. Old Marsh here had a rotten headache, and I had to do double duty on the dance floor. I can tell you, my footwork hasn't improved since I had to spend my Saturday mornings at Miss Penry's School of the Dance."

Persia felt an unaccountable lightness of spirit as Kathy went on to tell her husband that Chip had called half an hour earlier.

"He wanted Persia, but she was dead to the world." At Kathy's words, Persia slanted a hidden glance at Marsh, who was leaning in the doorway, hands in the pockets of his wet khakis, and a totally undecipherable expression on his lean, tanned face. "He spent last night at Ann's sister's house, and he and Ann are coming back here later on today."

"They're all patched up, then?" Tom asked, a slow grin blossoming on his bony features.

"I'm not sure," Kathy said hesitantly. "He said to ask Persia about it when I tried to pump him."

Tom turned expectantly to her, and Persia shrugged. "All I know is that he headed to Orangeburg last night to get her, and he said he was going to bring her here so that I could talk some sense into her like I did him."

"What on earth did you find to say to him?" Marilee jeered. "I didn't know any mere mortal spoke his language."

Conscious of Marsh's interested look, Persia leaned back in her chair and assumed a nonchalance she was far from feeling. "Oh, nothing in particular—I just made him realize how much he had to offer a woman. He was feeling a little—inadequate."

"Inadequate!" Marilee shrieked. "Is a rattlesnake inadequate? Is a cottonmouth inadequate?"

Amusement gleamed softly in Persia's dark eyes. A mutual admiration society. Did Chip suspect that his sentiments towards Kathy's best friend were returned?

Some twenty minutes later, Marsh caught her as she was headed for the tool shed. Cursing her idiocy in bring two suitcases full of glamorous new clothes and not one pair of jeans, she'd changed into a pair of washable pink slacks and a black halter.

"Hold on, Persia—can you spare me a few minutes?"

Bracing herself to meet his eyes, she replied, "I'm on my way to spade up the backyard before it gets too hot to work, so make it fast."

"Planning to bury a few bodies?" he taunted. In spite of the light tone, he looked slightly uncomfortable, and Persia gave in reluctantly.

"What did you want to talk about? If it's about last night, forget it. You'd been drinking. I certainly don't hold you responsible for it, if that's what you're worried about. And I'm not a snitch," she added piously.

"Come on—let's get out of here," Marsh said grimly, taking her arm and propelling her out the back door. He steered her along a pinestraw-covered path through the woods, his stride impatient as he headed for the old wooden bench that had been there for as long as Persia could remember. "Did you monogram this thing, too?" he asked when they reached their destination.

In a sudden flush of remembrance, Persia shook her head. She'd burn the blasted bench to the ground before she'd reveal the crudely carved heart on the bottom of the seat, with the initials P.K.A. and W.M.R.

Marsh dusted off a space and waited for her to take it. "I guess you were too young and I was too old for that sort of thing the last time we were here. Persia, what's all this business about Chip? Were you honestly just trying to—well, what *were* you doing out there on the pier, anyway?"

"On the pier?" she echoed slowly. Oh, dear heavens, had he been watching her impromptu performance as a marriage counselor? "Oh. That," she uttered lamely.

"Yes, *that*. From where I sat, it looked—well, you can see how anyone might misunderstand. In fact, I'm not sure I understand yet just what was going on out there. Care to enlighten me?"

Subduing an urge to jump and run, she stared fixedly at her short, unpolished nails. "Not really," she muttered, "but if you'll explain something to me, I'll tell you what that was all about."

"Deal," he said quickly, and she shot him a wary glance. She wasn't all that sure, on second thought, that she wanted any more of Marsh's "deals." Her plan for exorcizing an old fantasy was getting all twisted up in a reality she wasn't sure she could handle.

"Well, you see, Chip thinks he's a nerd."

"Discerning of him, I must say. That's one of the more flattering terms I can think of to describe him," Marsh interjected. "Sorry—go ahead."

"I guess I can't blame you for thinking that. He can be pretty brutal sometimes, but honestly, Marsh, it's just a matter of communication. You see, he's never been able to—I mean, not with people. I understand he speaks computerese in several different languages, but he got off on the wrong foot when he was in the first grade, and I don't think he's ever sorted himself out. I wondered at Ann's taste when she married him, but..." With Marsh's thigh so close to hers on the mossy old bench, and the memory of last night still raw on her mind, Persia was having trouble keeping her thoughts focused on Chip and his problems.

"Anyway, I finally caught on to what ailed him. He was a rotten brat, you know—he made my life pure hell, but it finally dawned on me that he was just a miserable little boy when it came to relating to ordinary people on a social level. He was afraid he'd bore them and they'd reject him, so he got in the first shot. So I kissed him."

"You kissed him!" Marsh exploded. "Forgive my denseness, but I fail to see how kissing a rotten brat fits into the picture. Or did you expect to transform him into a handsome frog?"

Turning to face him, she caught the glint of sunlight on his pale, unruly thatch. She turned away abruptly, unwilling to put her powers of resistance to the test on an empty stomach. With exaggerated patience, she said, "You see, he thinks no woman could possibly love him. He thinks he's got nothing to offer Ann. He's never even kissed anyone but her, can you believe it? So I showed him that— well, I let him see how..."

Marsh's square, capable hand traced a set of initials on the seat between them. "Yes? Do go on—I'm fascinated by this rationale of yours that kissing can make it better. What do you recommend for the everyday, run of the mill, harried businessman? Am I eligible for your particular brand of therapy?"

His eyes glinted with wicked amusement, and Persia took a deep, steadying breath and reminded him of their deal. "It's your turn now. Would you be so kind as to tell me what ailed you last night? And I don't mean that business upstairs, either. That was just—well, a combination of alcohol and propinquity. But what about that little attack at the foot of the stairs? I mean, you lit into me as if I were the cookie monster. Don't you think you were overreacting to a small bet about an insignificant matter? I mean, what difference can it make to you if I fall off the wagon?"

The corners of his mouth tugged downward as he studied her thoughtfully. Persia waited, pretending to a calmness she was far from feeling. Instead of getting better, it was getting worse. She'd thought that once she got accustomed to being around him, his spell would lose its power.

"You thought I was ticked off about our bet? Honey, did you really think I jumped on you about a little matter of a few forbidden calories?"

She lifted her shoulders, digging the toe of her platform sandal into the rich layers of leaf mold. "How should I know what it takes to set you off? We're practically strangers." Amazingly enough, it was true. She'd dreamed of him, idealized him, for years—the miracle was that the genuine article bore such a striking resemblance to all her homemade fantasies.

He took her hand, stilling the small agitated movements of her fingers. "Persia. I'd like to think we're friends. It's just that I thought—" He broke off, and she glanced at him, shaken to see a tide of color under the richness of his tan. "Believe it or not, I thought you were trying to take advantage of that poor devil's misery to seduce him," he confessed, "and then, heaven help me, I even thought you were making a play for Tom."

"Tom?" she echoed plaintively, crushed that he could even consider her in that light. "You thought that I—! Oh, Marsh, Tom's just like my own cousin. How could you possibly think I'd try to—that I'd even be interested in—"

"Yeah, sure, I know it's ridiculous. I don't know what got into me—maybe it was something I ate." His rueful grin curled warmly around her heart and Persia felt his magnetism tugging at her again. "Look at it from my point of view—I'd just watched you kissing one man, and then, before the dust had even settled, you were huddled up under the magnolia tree, batting your eyes at another one, throwing your arms around him."

Persia schooled her features to a reproving sternness. "I'm not exactly a batter of eyelashes, Marsh, in case you hadn't noticed." She blinked rapidly and considered the results.

"You've got the equipment for it," Marsh observed dryly.

"I guess it's all in the training. Mine's a bit lacking in some areas." Now that she considered it, she was amused at the whole misunderstanding. It was a relatively new role for her, and the most interesting aspect of the whole thing was Marsh's reaction. Was he always so protective of his friends?

"Actually," she told him, "Tom was telling me about

a surprise anniversary gift he has for Kathy. He had a few last minute doubts, and I was able to reassure him. So you see, it was much ado about nothing.''

"Oh, well—all's well that ends well.'' His words were light, but there was a speculative look in his eyes.

"As I said—a tempest in a teapot.'' She stood up and dusted off the seat of her pink pants. "I was on my way to get a shovel and start on the herb garden. Better get at it.'' The compulsion to dig up the ground had fled, but she felt a definite need to put some distance between them before she did something terribly foolish. It seemed that neither one of them had any great track record when it came to emotional stability.

"You don't know your Cicero from your Shakespeare,'' Marsh quipped. "But—as you like it.''

"English is your thing, not mine,'' Persia shot back with a playful wrinkle of her nose. "Do you know the difference between a pittosporum and a podocarpus?''

"Touché. Come fishing with us. It's too hot to work in the garden.''

Get thee behind me, Satan, Persia pleaded silently. A few hours on the lake with Marsh without the benefit of Marilee's companionship would be sheer heaven. She'd loved every minute of the last time. "No, thanks,'' she said casually. "I promised myself I'd do something about that overgrown mess in the backyard. No telling how many snakes those weeds are harboring.''

"I thought Kathy ordered us all off the premises. You don't want to inhibit the course of the great reconciliation, do you?''

"I'll stay outdoors until the all-clear signal.''

"They'll know you're out there. Besides, all that exercise can't be good for you. Come on, I'll bet you I catch three fish to your one, and I'll even spot you my favorite Diawa reel.''

"Have you ever seriously considered giving up the newspaper business for a career in gambling? It's a shame to waste such a natural inclination."

"It can't be a whole lot riskier, at that." Catching her hand, he swung it between them as they strolled back along the shaded path toward the house. "Tell you what, we'll take the barge and let Tom and Kathy have the Jon boat. Three hours, tackle, and location unspecified, and we'll outfish them in numbers and pounds, too."

She felt herself slipping. "Kathy's probably going to drive into town with Marilee."

"No, she won't."

"You're disgustingly sure of yourself," she taunted softly.

He shook his head in denial. "Honey, if you only knew how unsure I really am."

She hooted at that, tilting her face to the warming rays of the sun. Her composure grew at each small indication that the Marsh she'd idolized for so many years shared a few small failings with rest of humanity.

Kathy met them at the door. "They're in his room," she whispered fiercely. "Come on—we're going fishing, and we're going to stay gone whether they're biting or not!"

Persia relegated the herb garden to some future frustration. At the moment she felt on top of the world. "I'm not going without something to eat. I skipped breakfast, and if I know Tom, we'll be out there all day."

"I've already packed the food and drinks. Now hurry!" Kathy was still whispering, and Persia shot Marsh a laughing glance.

"This family's chock full of conspirators, in case you didn't know it."

"I'm beginning to realize it. Kathy, tell Tom this is his chance to try and get even for this morning. We'll team up against the pair of you. Two hours, no limits on tackle or location. Persia's going to bring me luck.'' He favored them both with a benign smile, and Persia felt another chunk of her resistance melt and flow away.

A pair of ice chests and two burgeoning baskets were already assembled on the end of the pier, along with two tackle boxes and an assortment of rods and reels. Persia looked doubtfully at her feet in the cork soled, macrame sandals. ''Couldn't I at least sneak in long enough to change my shoes?''

''No way,'' Kathy shot back. ''It's all very well to get them together again, but from now on, they've got to work it out alone. They can't come crying to you every time something happens.''

Tom loaded an ice chest in the Jon boat and Kathy handed down one of the baskets. Persia looked from Marsh to Tom, her eyes narrowing momentarily at what looked almost like smugness on Tom's dark face.

Had they planned this outing in advance? It hardly seemed likely in light of the fact that up until a few minutes ago, Marsh had considered her a walking mantrap.

She grinned at the mental image. Chip, of all people— and Tom! Good Lord, didn't the man know that no woman with a viable hormone in her body would look at another man when Marsh was around?

Chapter Six

The drone of the outboard was narcotic, but every nerve in Persia's body remained aggressively alert. She dropped the seatpad to the deck, choosing the side where the sun slanted under the canopy, and stretched out on her stomach, closing her eyes to the sight of Marsh's naked ankles between the soft, worn deck shoes and the tattered hems of his khakis. His pants were dry by now, but Persia's refractory imagination kept showing her pictures of Marsh as she'd first seen him this morning, in wet trousers, with the long, lean muscles of his powerful thighs clearly revealed under the clinging fabric.

After last night she'd felt like slipping away before daylight so that she wouldn't have to face him again. And then he'd been so decent and friendly that under the clear light of day, her embarrassment had gradually disintegrated. In spite of a few near relapses this morning, she'd thought she could handle it. Now she wasn't so certain.

Opening one eye, she studied his sprawling figure, with his long legs extended toward her, his arrogant head and those impossible shoulders of his silhouetted against the sky.

Why had she let herself in for this? Was she a glutton for punishment? Sighing, she closed her eyes. The vibrations of the hull and the warmth of the sun on her bare back gradually combined with the hopeless churning of her thoughts to send her into a light doze. She'd been awake til all hours after he'd left her room last night. The dregs of passion didn't blend all that well with Lady Baltimore cake and a guilty conscience. Now, half asleep, she felt something tickling the sole of her foot.

"Time to get busy, mate. We don't want the other team to get the jump on us, do we?"

Once more she cracked one eye open, this time to scowl at him. He was crouched beside her, his hand circling her ankle to lift her right foot.

"What is it about you and feet?" she challenged drowzily. "One way or another you're determined to hobble me, aren't you?"

She should have had her tongue amputated. Why on earth had she reminded him of that? If, after this two-week period was over, Marsh ever thought of her again, she'd just as soon be remembered for something other than her foot! That antique bed she slept in had doubtlessly been made in the days of the Pilgrims, when the stocks were considered a suitable punishment for misdemeanors.

"Did this happen last night?" Marsh asked, touching a bruise on her ankle with a tender, explorative finger.

"Mmm-hmm. Either I'm too long or my bed's too short. Isn't it about time for lunch?"

Touching the tip of his forefinger to his lips, he placed it on the lavender stain on her ankle, and then he carefully lowered her foot to the deck, smiling that crooked, heart-melting smile of his.

Persia felt her eyes flood with quick tears. She blinked furiously. Dratted hay fever! The pollen this time of year.... And she was hungry, too. Starvation always brought on an attack of collywobbles. "What's in the basket? Can we eat before we fish?"

"Dish it out, and I'll bait up. We can try minnows while we eat, and then I think I'll switch to a Mepps." He dropped the anchor and moved lithely to where the minnow bucket hung suspended over the side.

Persia crossed her ankles and rose to her feet in a single flowing movement. She'd practiced for years until she'd got it down pat—it had been one of her earliest ambitions. She tipped back the lid of the ice chest and unfolded the checkered napkin that covered the straw hamper. "Hmmm, there's beer, and...beer," she muttered. "Oh, nuts. I'll suck an ice cube."

"Come on, take a break. You said you'd skipped breakfast."

"If I'm going to break my diet again, it will be for something I crave more than beer." Her on-again, off-again diet. "Tom must have packed the drinks." Scowling, she delved deeper, unearthing chicken sandwiches, cupcakes, deviled eggs and cherry tomatoes. "Honestly, I think Kath has a troop of little elves who creep into the kitchen every night after we go to sleep and cook up mountains of food. I know she hasn't had time to make all this."

"We'd better check it out," Marsh said gravely. "Meet you downstairs on the stroke of midnight. If there's nothing doing, we'll look at the cake together, all right?"

The scowl fled, and she giggled. If he was going to be so likeable, what chance did a woman stand? Common sense alone should have made her keep her distance from him. If last night's conflagration had taught her anything, it was that she couldn't trust herself. Even with all her fantasies, she'd grossly underestimated his effect on her. Heaven help her if she got in the way of any more hands-on demonstrations.

She handed him a sandwich and a napkin full of eggs and tomatoes. Speaking briskly, she said, "We'll have to look at something else. I finished off the last of the cake last night."

"The truth will out," he intoned solemnly, lowering the minnow keeper over the side again. "That explains that shifty look in your eyes last night. I thought it was—"

"I *know* what you thought," Persia broke in, needing no reminders of that unfortunate chain of events. "Here, take your food before I use it for bait."

They fished and munched silently, drifting gently in the fitful breeze. Marsh baited her hook—she'd never quite been able to bring herself to hook a live minnow. After awhile she reeled in her line and gazed at the limp shiner helplessly. "I don't think I really want to be a party to this sort of thing. Worms are one thing—darling little baby fish are another. Maybe I'll try a plug later on."

"That darling little baby fish is probably someone's crochety old grandfather. And just because you can't tell one end of a worm from the other doesn't mean they can't— oh, hell! Now you've got me doing it!"

He grimaced at her and then turned his attention to his line. She wished she'd brought her sunglasses. At least she'd have been able to gaze at him without being quite so obvious about it. Digging her toes into the indoor-outdoor carpet that covered the aluminum deck, she nibbled on another tomato. What on earth had she been thinking of, to come along without even putting up a fight? If she had to sit here looking at that beautiful body, smelling that elusive blend of fish, tobacco and aftershave, and listening to that rich, raspy drawl of his, she was going to do something desperate.

"You'll starve to death on nothing but ice and tomatoes." He chided, ignoring the cork that was beginning to dance around nervously just off the starboard beam. "Have a sandwich. Have an egg."

"Something's scaring your minnow. I'll have an egg," she conceded grudgingly. Mayonnaise, sweet pickle relish, real bacon bits, and Lord knows what else was in it. Shifting her position slightly as an unusually cool gust of wind raised goosebumps on her back, Persia accepted a deviled egg and eyed it warily.

Marsh finished the last of his second sandwich and glanced at the brightly colored cork. "What are we going to do with all the fish? There's at least ten pounds of bass and bream in the refrigerator now."

Finishing the last bite, Persia leaned forward and helped herself to another egg. May as well be hung for a sheep as a lamb. "What's that old saw about everything I like being illegal, immoral or fattening?"

"I doubt very seriously that Kathy would harbor an illegal egg in her kitchen, but as to the morals of the particular hen that laid the eggs, I couldn't say."

"Cute. Could I have a swallow of your beer? I can't abide the stuff, but ice cubes just don't cut it, and there's nothing else."

Marsh watched the sleek muscles of her throat as she tipped back her head to swallow. It wasn't right for someone with such an appetite for life to have to limit herself. Society imposed too damned many limitations, already.

She handed him back the can, and he raised it to his lips, savoring the lingering warmth of her mouth. Lowering it again, he met her eyes.

"Persia, about last night—"

"We've already discussed it. I don't want to talk about it anymore."

"Damn it, Persia, we have to talk about it! I'm not in the habit of telling a woman off and then hopping into bed with her, no matter what you might think of me. I haven't even apologized to you yet."

"I forgive you, okay? You're off the hook. Speaking of which, I think you've lost your minnow."

"To hell with the minnow!" Impatiently, he reeled in the line, snapped the baitless hook to the shaft, and then laid the rig aside. "Now, about last night, I didn't get to explain about—"

"Marsh, if you explain one more thing, I'll—I'll hit you! It just—happened, that's all." Her voice had a glittery thinness to it that threatened to crumble at any moment. "It's certainly nothing to get upset about."

Frustration suddenly frayed the last threads of his patience, "Of course not! I suppose you make a habit of leaping into bed with strange men."

"You did the leaping," she reminded him. "I was sleeping peacefully. You barged in there drunk as a lord and fighting mad, and the next thing I knew I was fighting off an attack!"

"Fighting off an—! Oh, *ho*, so that's your story! Is that the way you and Patrick play the game?"

"I'm not playing games—and you can leave Pat out of it," she said coolly.

Marsh shot her a derisive look. But she was right about his being the aggressor. For some strange reason, he'd lost his sense of perspective. He'd gone upstairs in a foul mood, his temper inflamed by a few drinks, and before he'd known it, things had got completely out of hand.

"I reckon I did sort of forget my manners," he apologized.

"Manners! I've seen better manners in a—in a—!"

"Don't say it. Whatever you're thinking, I doubt if it's very ladylike."

"I'm not a *lady,*" Persia shot back, amusement beginning to dilute her irritation. "I'm a *woman.*"

A reluctant grin rearranged the angular planes of his face. "I'm not about to argue that particular point with you. All the same, honey, I'm sorry about last night. I guess I've been overworking lately. I know I've been out of sorts, and a few drinks didn't help my judgment. I think I owe you several apologies."

"One will be sufficient." Persia tried to ignore the feeling of emptiness that crept in to replace the amusement. She didn't want his apology, she wanted his kisses. She wanted far more than kisses from him, but she was certainly in no position to say so.

"Then you've got it. I don't see any need for you to upset your boyfriend over the matter. As you said, it didn't mean anything."

Forcing herself to press the spot that hurt most, she nodded. "Marilee, either. She's even more beautiful than she was at the wedding, isn't she? What do you think of this new interest of hers—is it just a hobby, or is she going into financial counseling professionally?"

Her eyes gleamed as brightly as polished gemstones, and Marsh found it increasingly hard to meet them. Damn it, it wasn't fair to compare the two women, so why did he keep on doing it? He'd been in love with Marilee since his freshman year in college—hadn't he? And Persia was just a good friend who happened to share a few interests— a friend of a friend, so to speak.

"What? Oh—that." He forced a lightness to his tone that he didn't feel. "I suspect the potential's been there all along, only it was disguised under that decorative surface of hers. Probably inherited it from her father. Let's talk about you for a change. Are you planning to stick to this landscaping thing of yours after you marry?''

Marry? Patrick? The irony of it flickered painfully in her eyes before she adjusted her mask of indifference. ''Sure, why not? I didn't get my degree just to decorate the wall. Besides, I'm too good to quit. I plan to leave my mark on Virginia for generations to come.''

As he studied her upturned face, half gilded by the sunlight, half in shadow, Marsh grew more and more morose. He only hoped this Patrick of hers wouldn't try to hold her back. Some men might feel threatened by all that strength and lovely vitality. ''So—when are you planning to be married?''

Swallowing hard, Persia shrugged. ''Pat's got a pretty busy schedule—you know lawyers. How about you and Marilee? I guess Tom and Kathy will be matron of honor and best man.'' Her smile was a work of art. ''Pity I won't be available. I'd love to be a bridesmaid, if only to get you to dance with me. You owe me one, you know.''

Marsh's laugh was a little late in coming, and even then, it wasn't particularly convincing. Persia had had far more practice at dissembling. Arms extended along the railing, she leaned back and gracefully crossed her legs. Her smile was more assured now. ''Of course, if you're planning to have hot-pink ruffles, you can definitely count me out.''

''No pink bridesmaids, and definitely no pink champagne punch.'' The teasing note in his husky drawl sounded slightly strained.

So it was official. Persia's spirits settled in a sodden heap about her feet and stayed there. If Marsh could discuss his wedding plans so readily, then it couldn't be that far off. Only now did she admit to herself that against all reason, she'd still held out a fragment of hope.

That dumb optimism of hers! She'd been so grateful for it after Pat's defection, telling herself that if she could only hang in there until the pain ended, she'd be all right. And it had worked. She'd buried herself in her job, taking on everything that came her way, no matter how insignificant, and spending weekends painting, repairing, and landscaping her own place.

So now she came face to face with the other side of the coin. All those silly daydreams of hers, all the adolescent fantasies she harbored—a harmless indulgence, she'd reasoned. Oh, she was good at it. She'd cultivated her skills as a daydreamer long ago to escape an unacceptible reality. As she'd grown older she'd continued to indulge herself, seeing only what she wanted to see, picking and choosing among the various versions of reality available to her. But she'd always prided herself on knowing the difference between the real and the imagined, and if one knew the difference, then where was the danger?

The danger, she acknowledged miserably, was that she was still a hopeless optimist. Stubbornly closing her mind to the facts, she'd gone through life expecting miracles. She'd visualized herself looking glamorous and attractive, and after awhile, it had happened—in a modest way, at least. She'd visualized falling in love with a handsome, successful man, and that had happened, too. Of course, it hadn't ended quite the way such dreams are supposed to end, but never mind.

So now the bubble had burst. And she had no one to blame but herself. She'd been blithely ignoring the facts, busily creating a cozy little scenario in which Marsh fell instantly and irretrievably in love with her. And it hadn't happened. Her optimism, her silly penchant for fantasizing, had finally played her false.

The trick now was to get herself back down to earth without injuring anything vital. Like her heart. And after all these years of living in castles in the air, she wasn't sure she could do it. On the other hand, she could get busy and start creating a vision of Persia graciously offering her sincere best wishes to Marsh and Marilee...

"Persia?"

She rejected the intrusion of reality into the blurred vision of a tall, lovely woman in a black linen sundress and a leghorn hat, her smile heartbreakingly beautiful as she extended a slender, manicured hand of congratulations.

"Persia, snap out of it. There's a squall blowing up. How about putting away the food while I take up the anchor and get us home?"

It had blown up faster than he'd expected. Starting the outboard and veering around a stand of dead cypresses, he was distracted from his task by the sight of her profile. She was seated in the bow, one knee curled under her, and her face was turned into the wind. As the last hairpin blew away, her hair streamed out behind her, reminding him of a wooden figurehead he'd once seen on a tall masted sailing ship.

Damn it, what had gone wrong? They hadn't straightened out anything! He'd deliberately arranged things with Tom so that he'd have this chance to be alone with her—to talk things over sensibly. After last night, he felt the need for a little coolheaded logic.

What had possessed him to go and pull a fool stunt like that? As if he didn't have enough on his mind already with his business situation the way it was. He'd been such a bear recently that his staff had practically railroaded him into taking this vacation. Besides which, he'd come down here to Pinopolis for the express purpose of getting himself engaged. So what had he done? At the first opportunity, he'd made a pass at another woman.

At Persia Abernathy, of all people—someone he'd taken an immediate and instinctive liking to, someone who was almost like—family. If a man had any last minute oats to sow, damn it, he had no business sowing them so close to home.

A scowl darkened his features. His hand gripping the controls ruthlessly, he rounded a channel marker at full throttle with only inches to spare. This lawyer of hers had damned well better be good to her, or he'd have some accounting to do. She hadn't a single man in her family left to look after her interests. Tom came as close as anyone, he supposed. He'd see that Tom checked him out, then—just to reassure himself.

His scowl darkened further as a shaft of lightning silhouetted her profile. God knows if Blake was anything like that bloodless pack of lawyers he'd locked horns with for the past four months, he'd have his hands full with a woman like Persia. She was...

He let out a frustrated sigh. Admit it—she was everything any man could want in a woman. Warm, open, passionate—sensuous and sensual in every respect. She had a wholesome attitude about her that pleased him enormously. Just looking at her made him smile and relax, and God knows, he'd done little enough of either recently.

But there was Marilee. He'd been crazy about her for so long that he'd even outgrown the heated excitement that went with it. But then, a man would be a fool to expect any fairy-tale romance in this day and age. He was no Prince Charming, and...besides, at their age...

It was just overwork and overworry—this peculiar restlessness he'd been feeling recently, this reluctance to actually settle things between them. Marilee had been hinting around, and he'd finally bought a ring, but for some reason, he was still dragging his feet. What the devil was he waiting for, for lightning to strike? Things like that didn't happen to guys like him. When it came to love, he was a realist—he'd learned the hard way.

A scattering of rain erased the shoreline for a few

minutes, reminding him that this was neither the time nor place for soul-searching. He was squeezing every bit of horsepower out of the Evinrude, but the squall was gaining fast. For several minutes he concentrated on getting them safely to port before the full force of the storm struck. Only when he caught a glimpse of Tom's red roof through the pines did he relax his grip on the controls.

His narrowed eyes were drawn reluctantly to the woman who was leaning into the weather with every indication of pleasure. Her face glistened with moisture as she peered eagerly through the premature gloom. God, she was even enjoying this squall. In some ways she was like a child, welcoming every new experience with open arms.

The way she'd welcomed him into her bed last night. It was going to be tricky. He'd have to handle things carefully if he didn't want her to mistake simple friendliness for something more. And after last night—particularly in light of Kathy's inadvertent disclosure—he couldn't dismiss the possibility. Underneath that breezy openness, she might still be harboring remnants of that school-girl infatuation.

Something inside him heated up at the thought, and he quenched it ruthlessly before it had time to ignite. At any rate, she was probably pretty vulnerable. She lacked the polished facade of so many other women he knew, women who were experts at looking after their own best interests. Might be a good idea to keep it light from now on—stick to non-threatening options. The diet thing, for instance. How lecherous could a man get when he was counting someone's calories?

The Jon boat was already in and tied up when he eased up alongside the pier. No sign of either fish or fishermen. Persia leaped out and started securing the lines while he handed out the ice chest and the empty picnic basket. They'd cleaned out the lunch basket—it had been a genuine pleasure to watch her eat real food for a change. If there was a single one of her five senses that woman didn't thoroughly enjoy, he didn't know what it was. As he busied himself closing tackle boxes and rounding up rods, he wondered absently what sort of music she'd like. Emotional rather than cerebral, he'd be willing to bet.

He checked the gas can, found it almost full, and tightened the cap. She was probably a marvelous dancer, too. He could picture her laughing as she moved uninhibitedly on a dance floor. It wouldn't occur to her to worry about something as trivial as mashing creases in a bouffant dress by dancing too close, or accidentally damaging the toes of her shoes by getting them trod on.

"You realize we got outfished," she reminded him, leaning over to take the fishing gear from his hands. Her pants clung translucently to her legs as the rain intensified. Out across the dark waters of the lake, lightning flashed almost continuously.

"How do you know? Maybe they got skunked, too."

Persia shook her head and grinned wetly down at him. "Maybe Tom did, but not Kathy. I've never known her to come back empty-handed."

"Women are just naturally more alluring than men. Doesn't have a thing to do with skill or ability. Come on, we'd better get out of here."

Loaded with gear, they made a dash for it. By the time they reached the shelter of the broad front porch, they were both soaked to the skin.

"Medusa," Marsh laughed, indicating the tendrils of dark hair plastered to her face and shoulders.

"Oh, thanks! On you, rain looks great—it's the first time I've ever seen your hair so neatly groomed."

Leaning the rods in a corner of the porch, Marsh stepped out of his sodden shoes. "Speaking of grooming, those pants of yours..."—His voice trailed off as he took in the sight of her once crisp pink slacks— "look great, too," he finished, a wicked grin lighting his dripping face.

"There's nothing like a little misfortune to bring out the sadistic side of some men," she derided, plucking at the clinging fabric. "This outfit will never be the same after today." She twisted the ends of her hair, and then knelt and wrung out the hems of her pants. "Maybe we'd better get someone to bring us some towels. I'd hate to ruin Kathy's floors."

"Coming up," Kathy sang out through the screened door. "We wondered what happened to you all. Marilee was all for calling out the Coast Guard." She handed over huge bath towels, and Persia began blotting off her face and arms. "Are you cold? Go on up and change and then come back and have something to drink. Persia, you can have a drink, can't you? You're not still on that silly diet, are you?"

"Yes." "No."

Their voices clashed, and Marsh and Persia looked at each other and burst out laughing. Marsh went first. "No what? *No,* you're not on the diet, or *no* you can't have a drink?"

"Don't confuse me. What did you mean by saying *yes?*"

Kathy looked from one of them to the other, and then gave Persia a shove toward the stairs. "You'd better get out of those wet clothes before you catch your death. We'll be in the living room when you come down."

They trooped upstairs together, hips jostling familiarly. "What did you mean by that, Marsh?" Persia looped the towel around her neck and squished moistly down the hall toward her room.

Pausing outside his own door, he said, "I meant *yes,* you are still on that silly diet. And *yes,* in a case like this, you can have a drink. We'll consider today as an official time out and start fresh tomorrow.''

"And last night," she reminded him, thinking of the cake she'd unknowingly devoured.

He nodded slowly, his expression not easily readable in the light of the single overhead fixture. "And last night," he agreed.

The door closed softly behind her, and he stood there staring absently at the white painted panels, seeing instead a pair of laughing eyes under a mop of darkly gleaming hair, flaring hips covered in two thin layers of clinging pink, and a tempting swell of damp, golden flesh above a thin black halter. She obviously wasn't wearing a bra— and he wished to hell she had been. If he was going to have to keep his thoughts under control, she was going to have to start wearing a few more clothes.

Outside, the squall made its way noisily off toward the coast. After an exuberant welcoming embrace, Persia settled down with Ann to catch up on all the news. Instinctively they avoided any mention of more personal matters. That could come later. Chip was tinkering with Tom's amplifier—it had been on the blink for months, according to Kathy. Marilee was leafing through the magazines and newspapers she'd brought back from town with her, and Persia was amused to see they were almost equally divided between fashion and finance.

As a weak glimmer of daylight filtered through the windows, Kathy stirred herself to start on dinner. She refused offers of help both from Ann and Persia. Marilee didn't offer.

Chip put down his tools and stared intently at his wife, and Ann, blushing, excused herself. A few minutes later Marsh and Tom left to dress the fish Tom and Kathy had caught. Marsh shot Persia a rueful glance, and she answered with an I-told-you-so smile.

Which left Marilee. Persia shifted her position in the deep comfort of the down cushioned loveseat, uneasily conscious of the fact that Marilee had laid down *The Wall Street Journal* and was looking at her speculatively.

"You really should do something about your hair, Persia. You have such a pretty face."

"Well, thanks—I think."

"No, really, I mean it. And if you took care of them properly, your hands would be lovely. Honestly, you've improved so much I hardly recognized you that first day. Marsh and I couldn't get over how much you'd changed. And I want you to know I think it's marvelous of you to keep plugging at it. It can't be easy." She laughed, a silvery, musical sound that for some reason, got under Persia's skin. "Especially with Kathy's cooking. Honestly, she's unbelievable. I wish I could steal her away and take her up to Chicago for a few days. I'd love to see her in a cook-off with Otto, Freddie's chef at the hotel."

"The Abernathy women were always known for their cooking," Persia observed tartly. Why did she keep feeling as if she were being patronized? Marilee was being kind and complimentary—wasn't she?

Persia made a deliberate effort to take the tactless remarks at face value. "It's not so bad—dieting, that is. I won't ever be really slender, but I've learned to live with it. At least I'm healthy as a horse, a fact that drives my doctor frantic. He's one of those men who runs every morning, and works out every night and gets sick at the mere thought of butter. He's probably the most joyless man I know."

"Yes, well—speaking purely as your friend, Persia, and I know you won't take it the wrong way, but those pink pants…"

"What about them? Other than the fact that they'll probably never be the same after today?"

"Well, with one of those pretty smock-type blouses, they wouldn't be so bad, but with a tight black halter, they make your hips look—well, of course, it's only my opinion, but they really make your hips look large."

Persia was no stranger to that "for-your-own-good" brand of sympathy. "My hips *are* large," she pointed out dryly, caught between anger and amusement. "At least compared to yours, they are. But my waist just happens to be a full ten inches smaller than my hips and my breasts, so relatively speaking, you might say I'm within the limits of normality." Grimly reminding herself of the penalty for murder, she murmured, "Your hair looks lovely, Marilee. I've always loved that color."

A small, satin-smooth hand fluttered up to touch the gleaming coppery cap. "It's my own color, you know. My mother's was the same shade when she was my age. And speaking of hair, darling, yours would be more flattering if you didn't pull it back in that awful braid. Even twisted up on top of your head, it's too—well, your features, the shape of your head..." She lifted her small shoulders in a gesture of helplessness. "Well, to be frank, on a woman your size, it makes you look pea-headed."

Short, well-kept nails drummed silently on the flowered chintz. Patience, Persia—a little polite mayhem might be satisfying momentarily, but it's not going to solve any long-term problems.

Persia stood. "I think I'd better go set the table. Unless you were going to do it," she added guilelessly.

Ann approached her first. Persia had wandered out onto the porch to avoid the bridge game going on inside. "Persia, I want to thank you," the slight, sandy-haired woman said quietly.

"Thank me for what?"

"I don't know what you did to him, but he's changed.

It's as if someone had taken a hammer and cracked the shell around him. What did you say to him?''

"It wasn't exactly what I said," Persia prevaricated.

"Then what did you do?"

Discretion prevailed as Persia decided not to describe the full treatment. "I let him know he wasn't a nerd—that he had a lot to offer a woman. Ann, he's got a terrible feeling of inferiority."

"Chip Gaillard?" Ann screeched. Then, clapping her hand over her mouth, she whispered hoarsely, "He's the most superior man I've ever met! I can't even talk to him he's so—so superior. The only place we ever communicated at all was in bed, and when that went sour, I couldn't take it. What does a man like Chip need with anyone—especially someone like me. I even flunked phys. ed., and believe me, that's not easy to do."

Briefly wondering at the source of her unexpected store of wisdom, Persia was able to make Ann see how desperately Chip needed her. "The plain fact is, he's handicapped by that brain of his. You've got to make allowances for his frustration. Ann, he wants to be able to communicate—he wants to be just like anybody else, but you've got to help him. You've got to meet him more than halfway. It won't be easy, even now that you know how much he loves you, but believe me, it'll be worth it."

Chip managed to catch Persia alone just before she went up to bed. "Persia, I wouldn't blame you for turning your back on me—I haven't always been especially polite to you."

"Noooo," she murmured consideringly, "in fact, there were one or two times when I wondered how it would feel to cut out someone's heart and use it for a doorstop."

Fingering his glasses nervously, he went on. "Yeah, well—technically, it takes more strength than you might imagine—unless you go between the xiphoid process and the costal carti—''

"Chi-ip!"

"Sorry." He grinned weakly. "Just joking. But Persia, seriously, I appreciate what you did for me. Ann's going to take me shopping and make an appointment for me for a—well, you know. A haircut."

"Hair styling," Persia corrected.

"Oh, okay—styling. But I promise you, if I don't come out looking like—like—''

It was obvious that he hadn't a clue as to who the latest male heartthrobs were. "How about Carl Sagan?" she suggested gently.

He scurried back inside soon after that. They'd traded bedrooms with Marsh, since the downstairs one was a single, like Persia's. Like hers, it had been added when the Gaillards had started bringing hoards of school friends down for the holidays.

An odd dreaminess seemed to afflict her as she swung herself slowly in the glider. The storm had long since passed, leaving in its wake a moon-washed sky and a deafening chorus of frogs. She hummed softly under her breath, closing her mind to the two-by-twoing going on all around her. The world wasn't made up of couples—it only seemed that way.

Marsh was ready and waiting for her at breakfast the next morning. "Back in harness again," he declared, placing before her a bowl of grapes and strawberries and a slice of dry toast.

"Do I have to?"

"I lost yesterday's wager—can't afford to let losing become a habit."

Marilee nursed her morning cup of weak tea, the only caffeine she allowed herself. "You're both being so childish. Diets! Honestly, when can we expect some decent, adult conversation around here?''

"Such as?" Chip chimed in. "Pass the cream, Annie."

"Such as—well, don't any of you watch the news? Do you realize what's been happening to foreign currency? I called Freddie last night, and he says the IRS won't allow me to swap Kruggerands for numismatic gold coins without paying a capital gains tax. Now I ask you, is that fair? It's not even logical!''

Her indignant glance touched on each one of them in turn, and Persia suppressed an urge to giggle. It was Chip who finally broke the silence. "That reminds me, Persia, I owe you five bucks for the gas money. Annie, have you got any money?''

Persia leaned back and howled. Vaguely she realized that she must sound like a fool, but she couldn't help it. It was so funny! The more she thought about it, the funnier it struck her, until finally, she wiped the tears from her eyes and caught her breath. "It's all a matter of perspective, I guess.''

Marilee looked offended, and Persia leaned forward and touched her hand. "I'm sorry, Marilee, it's just that..." She giggled and then tried again. "Don't mind me—I get slightly hysterical when my stomach's running on empty. It's just that for some of us, I guess five dollars is as important as a sockful of your Krugerrands.''

Besides which, she was once more uncomfortably aware of the pairing off around the table. Tom and Kathy, their chairs practically rubbing rungs, and Chip and Ann who were obviously holding hands under the table and trying to manage breakfast with one hand apiece. And Marsh and Marilee. He'd handed Persia her plate and taken his place beside Marilee as if he'd been doing it all his life. As if he'd go on doing it for the rest of it.

Sobering, Persia managed a trembling smile. "If no one

minds, I think I'll get started on the backyard this morning. Did I tell you what I had in mind, Kathy? I hope you don't mind—I just can't bear to waste all that loam on weeds.'' Besides which, she had a craving to dig that could land her in China, given enough time. Thank goodness there was only a little more than a week left of her vacation.

Chapter Seven

We're going to have a fish fry or open up a fish market," Kathy sighed resignedly. "At this rate, we'll need another refrigerator. It's a good thing you and Persia bombed out yesterday."

"Don't rub it in," Marsh retorted. He put his water glass in the sink and glanced out the back window. He'd been helping Tom all morning to clean the pinestraw from the gutters. "That's hot work," he commented.

"Yours or hers?" Kathy replied, nodding to where Persia was gathering up the last load of weeds. "Honestly, you all were supposed to be having a vacation."

"So were you," Marsh came back easily. He'd teased Kathy about her militant domesticity for years. Her argument had always been that if women were now considered liberated, then she had every right to do as she pleased, and cooking just happened to please her. Not cleaning— she made no excuses for having a maid three days a week, but when it came to her kitchen, she reigned supreme. No one he'd ever known had cared to take issue over the matter. For all her diminutive stature and her doll-like features, it amused Marsh to see her manage her six-foot-three-inch husband with no effort at all. They had a great relationship, and if he were half as lucky, he might soon be enjoying the same sort of thing, himself. Friends and lovers. What more could a man ask?

By dinnertime Persia was ready to drop. She'd spaded up every inch of the twelve-by-twelve foot square that had once been a kitchen garden. Not a single weed had survived her vigorous attentions. Plodding up the stairs for a much needed shower before she joined the others at the table, she wondered if it had been in vain.

Oh, not the landscaping results; she'd already estimated the bricks she'd need, and Tom had ordered them delivered first thing in the morning. But as a countermeasure to frustration and pain, she wasn't so sure it was going to do the trick. Marsh had been working within sight of her almost all day. He'd cleaned the kitchen gutters, moving agilely along the steep metal roof while she watched from the ground, her heart in her throat.

"Couldn't you at least use a ladder?" she'd called.

"Too much trouble to keep moving it. Don't worry, I'll clean up all the mess after I'm done."

The rich compost had been dumped unceremoniously down on her newly cleared ground, and she fully intended to make use of it to enrich the flower beds on each corner of her paved area. "I'll hold you to it," she'd warned. What she'd like to hold him to was herself. Shirtless, he'd clambered about under the broiling sun, sweat glistening on his deeply tanned back, and she'd been torn between fear for his safety and irritation at the distraction. What good did it do her to try to eject him from her mind when

he persisted in planting himself right where she could see
him every minute of the day?

At least she'd be able to fit into the one really swishy
party dress she'd brought with her, she consoled herself as
she dried off hastily and reached for her underwear. At
this rate—eating like a rabbit and slaving away in the
yard—she'd be ten pounds thinner at the end of the two
week period.

Did that mean she lost the bet, or won it? How the devil
had she ever got herself involved in such a hare-brained
scheme? And with Marsh, of all people! As if it weren't
enough just to share a house with him in the company of
five other people, she had to let herself in for an additional
intimacy.

Stepping into her oyster linen pants, she twisted around
anxiously and peered into the mirror. Not bad. Just to be
on the safe side of Marilee's critical eyes, she put on a
black and white tunic. It came down far enough to cover
a multitude of sins.

Working swiftly and automatically, she swirled her hair
up and anchored it with a comb and a few strategically
placed pins. And then she took it down again, back
combed furiously, and then piled it up once more. Pea-
headed, indeed!

"—tomorrow night," Kathy was saying when Persia
joined them at the dinner table. "I'll call around and see
who's here, and we'll borrow a few grills. I'll make gallons
of potato salad—remind me to get some vidalia onions and
a jar of capers. I could do some of those cheese and sausage bonbons and—let's see…oysters and chicken livers
with bacon and mushrooms, and—"

"I give up, I surrender," Persia wailed. "Honestly Kath,
the Geneva Convention has specific laws against this sort
of treatment. If you do anything in chocolate, I'm going
home!"

''Oh, hush up and eat your celery,'' Kathy taunted. ''Chip, is the thingmadoodle fixed yet? If it is, we could set it up outdoors for dancing, couldn't we?''

''The thingmadoodle,'' he repeated blankly. And then, ''Oh. *That* thingmadoodle. If you have a tape, I'll check it out after dinner.''

Persia savored the last fragment of steamed broccoli. She'd insisted on broiling her own serving of chicken breast, leaving off all the buttery goodness Kathy used with such a lavish hand. It had been dry and stringy, but she'd devoured every morsel.

Tom brought in the cassette carrier from his car after dinner, and Ann and Persia shuffled through the selection, exclaiming now and then when they found a favorite. ''Oh, goody—*I Love Beach Music,* by the Embers. And here's the one I learned to shag to. Remember 'Sixty Minute Man'? I polished more dorm floors at Mary Washington dancing to that song.''

Comments came freely from everyone except Marilee, who was on the phone at one end of the long living room. Tom and Marsh tried to recall the name of a group that had been popular when they'd been at U.S.C., and Ann, who was Persia's age, reminded her of an incident at one of the favorite high school hangouts.

''Can't prove it by me—I never set foot in the place,'' Persia replied equably. Her father had adamantly refused to allow it—not that she'd been in great demand at any of the social events.

''You didn't miss anything,'' Chip put in. ''A lot of birdbrains sacrificing their hearing to throw their sacroiliacs out.''

''Chip,'' Persia murmured warningly.

''Sorry,'' he grumbled. ''but you know I can't handle that stuff.''

''It's not too late to learn. Ann, take him in hand.''

Tom put on a tape and reached for Kathy. "Remember this?" he whispered loudly, humming off key. "'Miss Grace,' by the Tymes? Remember that night at Myrtle Beach when you got locked out?" He leaned over to rest his chin on his wife's head.

With a half expectant look on her face, Ann moved closer to Chip, but he remained stubbornly rooted to one spot. "Go on, Chip," Persia prompted. "It's painless."

He eyed her balefully, and she turned impatiently to Tom and Kathy. "Would you please demonstrate for your baby brother? Ann can't lug a dead weight around with her all night, and he hasn't a clue!"

Tom was perfectly willing; unfortunately, he was hampered by a terrible sense of rhythm. Persia turned in desperation to Marsh. "Can't you do something? Cut in on them. Tom dances like he's trying to stomp out a grassfire."

"I heard that crack, woman," Tom called threateningly. "If you're such an expert, let me see you get out here and do any better." Turning toward her, he opened his arms, while his wife stood by giggling.

"I'd sooner dance with an iguana," Persia jeered. From the other end of the room, Marilee signaled impatiently for quietness, and Marsh reached over and lowered the volume fractionally. Then he turned to Persia. "Come on, honey, let's show 'em how it should be done. Or are you afraid I'll show you up with my skill and grace?"

"Stand back, everybody, this is going to be a center ring attraction," Persia promised. Her heart had already shifted into high, and her eyes sparkled with the hidden fire of black opals. She took the proffered hand and allowed Marsh to lead her to the middle of the impromptu dance floor.

The tape was one of the better known groups, taped live. The familiar beat, the intermittent applause, all combined to infect Persia with an excitement that had her laughing provocatively up into Marsh's face. Barefooted, she was several inches shorter than he, but their steps matched beautifully. She knew a fleeting wish that they were dancing something other than the lazy shuffle that had been so popular in the region for as long as she could remember.

Marsh moved in behind her, smoothly carrying on the STEP-step-step, KICK-step-step, CROSS. She felt the length of his body bracing hers. He came in so close that the front of his thigh moved against the back of hers. Instead of placing a hand on each of her hips, his arms reached around her middle, and for a breathless moment she fancied she could feel the beat of his heart against her back.

And then they turned, and she caught sight of Marilee. Her face was paper white, and two spots of unaccustomed color burned in her cheeks as she slammed the phone down into the cradle. Persia's steps faltered, and she blundered into Marsh. He caught her, hugging her against him. His laughter rang out in the room, and then he planted an impulsive kiss on her lips.

"Lord, I'm too old for this sort of thing! Can this woman dance, or can she dance?" he exclaimed proudly. He'd known instinctively that she'd be marvelous.

"She can dance," Chip agreed indifferently. "Is that what I have to learn to do?"

"Care to give it a try?" Persia asked, feigning enthusiasm. Poor Chip looked as if she'd suggested walking the plank. "Think of it as a mathematical equation. Once you get the formula down, you'll be fine."

"I analyzed it pretty thoroughly," Chip told her morosely. "I'll try it sometime when I'm alone."

"Alone! It's not supposed to be a solo performance," Persia informed him disparagingly. "The object is—oh, forget it. Ann, he's all yours. Any man intelligent enough to invent a gizmo that has three foreign countries panting after him can learn a simple dance step. Take him off somewhere and motivate him.''

The evening disintegrated soon after that. Marilee, her lips tight and her color higher than usual, collected Marsh and led him out to the darkness of the screened porch. Tom and Kathy had already wandered off, mentioning something about seeing if the barbecue grill had rusted through yet.

Marsh sprawled in the glider, one arm extended along the cushion to rest lightly on Marilee's shoulder. The cool night air was welcome after all that exertion. It had been years since he'd done anything more than dinner and cocktail dancing of the most perfunctory sort. He'd forgotten how much fun it could be. For exercise, he'd match a fast shag against jogging any day.

''—so Freddie said that if I can get my hands on some of Daddy's trust fund and sell of part of the securities he settled on me when we were married, I'll have enough for five thousand shares. And with a return projected at—''

Funny—just yesterday he'd been wondering what sort of music she'd like. Not, of course, that beach music would be the extent of her musical tastes. She moved beautifully. Totally uninhibited, she'd laughed up at him as if they were sharing something far more intimate than a dance.

''The trouble is, I can't clip the coupons until July, and by that time, the price might have risen. Now, I was thinking that if you—''

Of course, it was probably his imagination. Just because, according to Kathy, she'd once been infatuated with him— just because he couldn't look at her without thinking of certain passages from the *Kama Sutra*...

''—have to hold it for a year and a day to qualify for long-term capital gains, and if the economy takes another dip, we might have to hold off selling even longer, but Freddie says we can—"

It was a wonder he hadn't broken his neck up on the roof today. He'd had trouble keeping his eyes on what he was doing, much less his mind. She'd gone at it as if she'd been digging for gold, sweat gleaming on her back and her thighs, that marvelous hair of hers tumbling a little more every time she shook it out of her eyes. By the end of the day, she'd had more dirt on her than she'd left in the backyard.

And he'd give everything he owned—which, at the moment, was negligible—to bathe it away. With slow and lingering strokes. When she'd gone upstairs he'd watched her long, sweat-polished legs take the steps and he'd experienced a few muscular flickers in his own body—and not in his legs, either.

"—thought it would be a marvelous opportunity for you. I mean, I hate not to include Tom, but I doubt if he could swing it anyway, and Freddie said I couldn't tell a soul. But I could let you in on it for a measley little old ten thousand. I mean, after all, since we're practically..."

Marsh turned his head slowly and studied the cameolike perfection beside him. "Ten thousand *what?*"

With barely concealed impatience, Marilee repeated her offer. "Ten thousand dollars is the minimum investment Freddie recommends. Marsh, haven't you even been listening? It's that Canadian mining company I told you about. Copper, Marsh—copper, zinc, cobalt. Freddie says copper stocks always slump during a recession, but they're among the fastest to recover once the cycle takes an upward swing."

He managed to pull together his full attention and focus it on the slender, exquisite woman sharing the glider with him. It was a little like rounding up a herd of wild horses and getting them to do a slow waltz. "Now—I gather you want me to invest in some mining outfit, right? And at the propitious moment, good old Freddie will send up a rocket and we'll sell out and all live happily ever after."

"Don't be an absolute ass, Marsh—of course there's more to it than that."

"Oh, yeah—we split the take with a few brokers and Uncle IRS. Sorry, honey, but I'm afraid I'll have to pass. There's only one way I could come up with that sum in a hurry, and I doubt if you'd care for it."

"Are you still worrying about finding enough to buy out Timmon-Edwards? Cash something in. Surely you kept enough of your portfolio in negotiables to be able to take advantage of something like this."

"I think you overestimate me, Marilee," Marsh said quietly. His collar felt suddenly as if it were choking him. Inserting a finger in it, Marsh realized that he was wearing an open-necked knit shirt. "Timmon-Edwards has a lot of potential, but it will be at least three years before it can possibly begin to show a profit, and even then—"

"So you've got a cash-flow problem at the moment. You could borrow, and at half a percent above prime, you'd still stand to clear—"

"Marilee. Honey." Marsh enunciated very carefully, wondering if she really thought he was in the same income bracket as his father. "You don't seem to understand. Every cent I have is tied up in those newspapers. It's no hobby with me, Marilee—I can't afford hobbies on that scale. If this deal goes through, I'll have seven weeklies with what I've got now, and at least three of them are going to have to be completely overhauled, from editorial to circulation departments. To get decent staff, I've got to be able to pay for it. They've been muddling along for years with one marginally competent editor, a handful of high school stringers, and a few local club secretary reports."

"But if you took out a loan—" Marilee suggested patiently.

"I'm already extended past the limit. Everything I've got is on the line, and if the bank won't give me an extension, then I might have trouble buying a subscription, much less another publishing firm."

"But what about your father? Good Lord, you're his primary heir—why can't he turn loose of some of your inheritance now, when you need it?"

This was not something Marsh enjoyed discussing. Still, he supposed that if anyone had a right to know, it was Marilee. "I'm not Dad's heir, honey—primary or otherwise. I told you I had a half-brother, remember? John Paul's thirteen now, and he's—well, Dad and Charlesia try to pretend everything's okay, but John Paul has a—a learning disability. He has brain damage. Dad and I agreed that his affairs should be arranged to look after Charlie and John Paul if anything should happen to him."

The hand that had rested along the back of the glider dropped between them, and he stared at it as if it belonged to someone else. He had a strange feeling that what was said in the next few minutes would have a bearing on the rest of his life. "I don't need Dad's money, Marilee. I've done pretty well on my own—what's even more important, I like what I do. I'm good at it. Once I'm over this hump, things should begin to smooth out again financially."

The space between them suddenly seemed to expand. In an impeccable accent that was totally devoid of emotion, Marilee asked, "Are you certain you're not forgetting something—perhaps some, ah—jewelry? Your mother might have left you some nice pieces, or you might have picked up something as an investment. What about this—this 'one way' you mentioned?"

Thinking of the emerald and diamond ring he'd sold his last tax-exempt security to buy, he smiled a little grimly.

This was supposed to be a joyous, long-awaited occasion for him. So how come the ring was still upstairs in the corner of his suitcase? Damned if he knew.

"Mother's jewelry went to her sister. No, honey, I'm afraid you and Freddie will have to take this ride without me."

"But—but what about—? Oh, forget it!"

There seemed nothing more to say. About finances—about anything. For several long moments the creak of the glider and the ambiguous sounds of the summer night reigned supreme. When Marilee spoke again, her voice registered a brittle sort of cheeriness.

"Well, I guess I'll say good night. Kathy has this insane idea of throwing some sort of neighborhood brawl, so I'll need to keep up my strength."

She leaned over and kissed him lightly on the cheek, and some streak of perversity made Marsh reach for her. She didn't try to avoid his lips, but neither did she participate. It was as though she weren't even there. They were just going through the motions, and suddenly he was immensely saddened. He'd thought they could make a go of it, despite all that had happened.

His mind worked with amazing clarity even as his mouth moved slowly on hers, and then he eased her away from him and sighed.

Was this it? Was this all he could expect from now on? Then why bother? "I'm sorry I can't play in the same league as you and Freddie, honey."

Brushing the collar of her dress where his hand had rumpled it, Marilee shrugged. "You don't know what you're missing, Marsh. It's an exciting game—money. When you're good at it—and I am—it can be unbelievably stimulating."

Studying the cool perfection of her pale features, Marsh wondered if she'd always been this way. Had he been so damned young and green that he'd misread her all along, or had she changed as she grew older? They'd been apart a lot of years. Maybe too long. Or maybe his tastes had changed.

"Persia why couldn't you have come up with that fantastic design for the backyard before now? It would have been perfect for this sort of party." Kathy jammed a flowered potholder into the pocket of her matching apron. "Have you seen Tom? He was supposed to get another bag of ice. Oh, there's the Kelseys—I haven't seen them since last summer. Be a sweet and take over here for me, will you? Just spoon the sauce over the fish and then seal them up in foil."

Persia stirred and spooned, spread and sealed. The stack of silver packets beside her grew. Periodically Ann or someone else would come and take away a trayful to be placed on one of the three charcoal grills.

"On the sauce, are you?" Marsh teased, coming up silently behind her. "How much have you tasted?"

Grinning over her shoulder, Persia licked her lips. "Did I leave some evidence?"

Marsh's brows flattened in sudden tension. He was standing so close to her that she could detect a faint drift of his aftershave. If she should happen to faint, he'd be forced to catch her. She'd never fainted in her life, and, she concluded reluctantly, she was hardly likely to start now. Besides, a genteel swoon lost most of its effectiveness if one knocked over one's intended savior. She'd almost done that once, ten years ago. It wasn't an act she particularly cared to repeat.

"Here," she said instead. "Taste this and tell me how marvelous it is. Sour cream, dill, lemon juice, mustard and slivers of almonds. Isn't it revolting?"

Dutifully, he opened his mouth, and she tipped a spoonful of the delectable sauce onto his tongue. He savored it thoughtfully. "Hmmm—one of Tat's recipes? Just a bit heavy on the mustard for my taste. What do you think?"

"Oh, no, you don't," she chuckled. "You're not catching me with any of your dirty tricks. I haven't taken a single cheating bite all day, and I don't intend to now."

"Not even those chocolate things over on the dessert table?" he asked skeptically.

Persia closed her eyes tightly. "*Don't*... say that word. Didn't you know that every woman has her price? Mine's chocolate-covered cherries, all swimming in liqueur. I'd kill for one right now."

The crowd was increasing every minute. Children played tag among the legs of the adults, and three white-haired women sat fanning gently under a magnolia tree, looking cool and elegant in their afternoon pastels.

"Where's Chip? Somewhere gritting his teeth, I'll bet."

Marsh allowed his eyes to stroke the velvety texture of her nape as she lowered her head over the table. Other appetites began to stir. "At the moment, he's hooking up the speakers on the side porch. Do you know you look lovely in that deep bluey green thing?"

At his unexpected compliment, she ducked her head and busied herself with the last few filets of bass. "Thank you. Just a little something I ran up on my charge account. How many people are here, anyhow? I don't think I know a single soul."

"Everybody in Pinopolis, half of Monck's Corner, and a few from Eutawville, I think. Everybody brought somebody." He nibbled a sliver of almond and then reached for another one, and she cracked his knuckles with a spoon.

"That's not sanitary."

"Look who's talking sanitary! You're the only woman I've ever known who can eat with one hand and lay bricks with the other. How about taking on an apprentice tomorrow? It might come in handy to learn another trade.''

''You're on. I was wondering how I was going to finish before I have to go back home.''

''So Virginia's home now, hmm?''

She spread the last side of fish and neatly double-folded the edges of foil around it. ''Yep. I guess I'll always feel closer to South Carolina, but Virginia's where my job and my house are.'' She looked around helplessly for something on which to wipe her hands, and Marsh took her wrists in one hand and reached for a roll of paper towels, dampening one of them.

''Not to mention your lawyer friend,'' he reminded her as he daubed at her fingertips.

That foolish vanity of hers! She'd told one impulsive lie, born of a silly need to protect her pride, and now she was stuck with it. Why not simply tell him the truth? What was so disgraceful about a broken engagement?

The disgrace, she jeered silently, was that if she confessed, she'd have to explain why she'd bothered to lie in the first place. Out of the frying pan with a vengeance!

''You two come and start the dancing, will you?'' Kathy urged, ducking around a large man in a clerical collar who was talking Labrador Retrievers with a couple from Eutawville. ''Somebody's got to go first, and Tom's dragged Marilee off to help him look for those old kerosene lamps for later on.''

''Dancing!'' Persia wailed. ''But I'm starving!''

Kathy shrugged flippantly and disappeared, and Marsh said, ''Take a northeasterly heading and turn right just past the woman in the orange bed sheet. I'll feed you first, and then we'll dance.''

''Chocolate?''

''No chocolate.''

Her hunger had nothing at all to do with food. The

thought of dancing with Marsh to the slow, dreamy music that was just now drifting out from the porch was sweeter than any chocolate. It was enough to dry up her appetite forever. That was no shag Chip was playing this time. That was cheek to cheek stuff, and she wasn't sure she could hang on to her dignity with his arms around her and that quirky smile of his just inches away.

Wild horses couldn't have held her back. In spite of her better judgment, in spite of Marilee and poor uninvolved Patrick, she knew she was going to wrap her arms around his body and match her thighs to his, and let nature take its course.

"Well come on—if I'm to be Queen of the May tonight, let's get on with it." She laughed up into his face, freely abandoning any pretense of reluctance. Prudence was not her style.

They waded through a noisy group talking politics, and Persia almost tripped over a small boy who was zooming a toy truck along the edge of the driveway. Unconsciously, she bent and touched the small, sweaty head of curls as she brushed past. As they passed the large woman in orange and headed for a table laden with an assortment of raw vegetables and dips, she muttered, "More vegetables—I should have known. And it's not a bed sheet. It just happens to be a very chic, very expensive tent dress."

"Is it supposed to be fetching? You don't go in for that type of thing, do you?"

"Not since I discovered my waistline." Homing in on the tray of low-calorie delights, she grinned over her shoulder at him. "If you've got it, flaunt it, I always say." She popped a tiny cherry tomato into her mouth and reached for a broccoli florette.

"Here, try this," Marsh murmured seductively, dipping a sliver of cauliflower into something green and creamy.

"I hope you know what you're doing." She leaned forward and bit off the tip of the proffered treat, and he dunked the remaining end back into the avocado dip and munched it with every indication of enjoyment.

"Would I encourage you to sin? The dip makes it a green vegetable. According to the diet sheet, green vegetables are allowed in unlimited amounts." He offered her the last bite, and she took it from his fingers. He immediately set out to compose another *piece de resistance*. This time it was carrot sticks dipped in curried cream cheese, and she let herself be led hopelessly astray. It wasn't that she was hungry—it was just that she found it impossible to refuse anything Marsh offered.

I want this woman. The words burned inside him with a white-hot intensity. He fed her a benne seed wafer loaded with chopped shrimp and capers in sour cream, and then licked a smudge of the cream from his fingers. He'd like to smother her in cream, and then spend a lifetime removing it. Then he'd try honey.

"This is another moratorium, you realize," he murmured. "Parties and fishing trips don't count."

"You're a dreadful influence, Marsh. I'd be big as a house if I let you feed me much longer."

"No you wouldn't," he rejoined calmly. "I'd find ways of working it off. Dancing—a few select indoor sports. Come on, let's wrap ourselves around that old Glenn Miller tune, shall we? I never knew dancing could be so much fun."

There had to be an ordinance against anything so sinfully sweet. Persia buried her nose in the side of Marsh's throat. Under the cover of her long, billowing skirt, she was barefooted. The gauzy cotton gown was caught above the waist with lime and lavender ribbons that floated out around her as she pivoted, her inner thigh braced against Marsh's.

"You look like Maid Marian in that getup," he murmured against her hair.

"How about Maid Persia?"

"Is that an invitation?"

Closing her eyes, she held her breath and let herself flow with the sensuous movements of his arms, his body, his long, muscular legs. The subtle, woodsy scent of him teased her nostrils, and under her hands, the heat of his body escalated until her palms were damp. She gave one fleeting thought to such negligible matters as engagements, pending or broken, and then she gave herself over to the exquisite sensation of being held in his arms, swaying in an ever decreasing circle as the rest of the world slowly faded away.

Don't think about it—just enjoy it, Marsh told himself. He gathered her softness still closer against him, and his hand fell below her waist to the curve of her hips. He closed his mind to all the reasons why he had no business being here. They danced through the cool green shadows of the magnolias and found themselves on the other side of an overgrown ligustrum hedge. A tenor sax reached out to bring them one last haunting note, and then the noise of the party faded into the background. Against the sound of increasingly ragged breathing, their movements ceased altogether. Tension held them silent for one fragment of eternity, and then he whispered hoarsely, "You know what I have to do."

"I know." She lifted her face, meeting him halfway. A hot, sweet weakness invaded her bones, and she sagged against him, accepting the aggressive masculinity of him. Inside her body, icecaps were melting, valleys were flooding, earthquakes were rending her apart. Daringly, she explored the small irregularity of his teeth with the tip of her tongue.

I know, I know, the voices echoed plaintively inside her. Hadn't she always known? Hadn't he?

Her hands moved restlessly over his back, savoring the rich resiliency of his muscles. They dropped lower, to bite into the hardness of his taut buttocks. In a saner moment, she'd have been aghast at her own actions, but she'd never been farther from sanity in her life. A moratorium, he'd said. *Until tomorrow, then, my sweet fantasy.*

When she swayed in his arms, and then laughed breathlessly about it, he lowered her to the ground. "Clover," she murmured absently, pulling him down on top of her. "Probably bees, too."

He tugged aside the thin covering and bared her shoulder. Burying his lips in a hollow at the side of her neck, he muttered, "You can't scare me off that easily."

The words vibrated down her spinal column. She shuddered as her heightened senses attenuated to the breaking point and shimmered there. Twisting her head helplessly in the cool, damp bed of clover, she felt his hands at her ribbons, felt the gentle pressure ease as he loosened each tie. Throwing out words in a breathless attempt to stay the inevitable, she whispered, "Without the ribbons, it's a tent dress. Not very fetching, remember? Ah, Marsh, you know we can't do this—please."

The last band of grosgrain dropped away, leaving the soft material to fall around her in loose folds. He felt beneath her for a zipper. "How do you get in and out of this thing?"

"Over my head, but Marsh, we can't! The people— they're all over the place. Any minute now—"

"Any minute now I'm going to self-destruct," he growled.

"This is madness!"

She took the full weight of him for an instant, savoring the feel of hard, angular masculinity pressed intimately against soft, rounded femininity. Then, as if reluctant to relinquish the symbolic dominance, he eased to one side. In an effort to control his runaway pulse, he closed his eyes tightly and drew in a deep, ragged breath. She gazed at his mouth, the firm lips pulled sharply against his teeth. Against the angular cheekbones, his eyelashes fanned out in an unexpectedly delicate pattern. Something inside her whimpered and reached out.

This was Marsh. This was no fantasy, no figment of an overromantic imagination, this was a flesh and blood man, from the overlapping tooth to the tiny scar on his chin, to the eyelashes that were as soft and feathery as a child's. This was the man she loved so deeply it was slowly destroying her.

"This is crazy," he repeated under his breath. And then he turned to her again, his green eyes almost swallowed up by the dark nuggets of his pupils. "Persia, do you believe in..."

"Do I believe in what, Marsh?" Was that trembly thread of a voice hers? With his face hovering so close, his eyes probing relentlessly, she believed in everything. Totally vulnerable to him, she waited for him to go on.

He groaned. Closing his eyes on something that looked almost like pain, he took her mouth in a harsh kiss. Teeth scraped against teeth as he ravaged her, twisting her lips ruthlessly, crushing her deeply into the bed of clover. His hand found its way inside the low neck of her dress, and he burrowed his fingers into the curve of her breast. She flinched, and immediately his touch softened. His tongue assuaged the small wounds his mouth had inflicted, while sensitive fingertips caressed her, erasing his fleeting harshness.

He was being torn apart by something. She knew it instinctively, and she ached for him. Whatever it was, she hadn't the right to ask him to share it, but if holding her could help, even for a little while...

Oh, God, don't lie to yourself, Persia! Not now—not anymore. Take what you can from him, but don't deceive yourself that its for any altruistic reason. Take what he's offering and run!

But this was neither the time nor the place. As the sounds of the party intruded, the swift tide of passion that seemed to rise each time they touched, began to ebb again. It was replaced by a fragile mixture of wariness and concern. As if he'd forgotten it, Marsh's hand still covered her breast. Without moving it, he lifted her head and re-settled it onto his shoulder. His breath stirred tendrils of hair on her forehead as they lay under the canopy of green, listening to the gentle noise of the party—the laughter and the music, the buzz of conversation and the bursts of shrill laughter. When he spoke, most of the tightness had gone from his voice, but she was acutely aware of the tension in the fingers that covered her breast.

"You know, don't you, that I've grown awfully fond of you, Persia?"

Fond. One was *fond* of Dickens, *fond* of maple syrup. She didn't want him to be fond of her—she wanted him to be *wild* about her, to lust after her, to ache for her! "Have you?" she inquired with seeming mild disinterest.

"We've gotten to be pretty good friends, in spite of a rather unfortunate beginning, wouldn't you say?"

Lifting her head slightly, she looked pointedly at the hand that was still half inside the neck of her dress. "You mean we're bosom pals?" she asked dryly.

In a quick motion, his hand slipped deeper, flattened on her ribcage, and then climbed the slope of her breast once more. It hesitated for one liquid moment as his palm slid over the taut nipple, and then it was withdrawn. "Would you believe I'd forgotten where I'd left that hand?"

"No."

"Smart woman." They remained silent for some time. After awhile Persia tilted her head to peer up into his face. His eyes were closed, but the white lines of strain at the corners of his mouth made her know he was not sleeping.

"Marsh? Don't you think we'd better get back to the party? Someone's bound to wonder where we are and come looking."

His sigh seemed to echo up from some desolate valley. He smiled, and then he opened his eyes and turned to gaze down at her. "I reckon you're right, but as unlikely as it sounds, this is as close to complete relaxation as I've come in a long, long time."

Play it cool—keep it light. "I'm not sure if that's a compliment or a very subtle insult."

Easing her head from its nest on his shoulder, he turned to face her, propping his head on his hand. "It's a compliment, lovely lady—and you know it, too. For some reason I've been having trouble sleeping lately. Not to mention a little trouble controlling my baser instincts when I'm around you." His grin was as beguiling as ever, but his eyes held a wintery light.

Out of a dozen clever responses Persia could have made, she chose evasion. "Oh, I don't know—you tame down easily enough at the first scent of food. And I'd say from the way things are beginning to smell, that dinner's about ready, wouldn't you?"

Pretending a vital interest in locating her scattered ribbons, she avoided his searching glance. Desperately she tried to tell herself that she was glad he'd cooled off before they got too deeply involved. It was a little hard to hear the voice of common sense, however, when someone inside her was whimpering like a wounded animal.

Chapter Eight

Shutting out the awareness of pain, Persia drifted numbly through a kaleidoscopic blur of color, sound, and movement. Somehow she managed to get through the next few hours without giving in to the urge to cry and throw things. There was no place to hide—people wandered in and out of the house, and the children had discovered the old bench in the clearing out back.

Plastering a social smile on her face, she poured iced tea and served plates and said, yes, it was an early spring. She collected used plates and glasses and disposed of them and said no, she really didn't think the azaleas had been at their best this year.

Her poise was nearly wrenched away from her when she blundered into Marsh and Marilee, strolling arm in arm toward the driveway, where several couples were dancing.

"Oh, hi," she greeted with shattering cheerfulness. "Did you all finally locate the lamps, Marilee?"

"Obviously."

"Obviously," Persia echoed dully. There were half a dozen Aladdin lamps in evidence. Her glance skittered away from the grape green eyes to another pair that were several shades darker, several degrees warmer. "I think the crowd's beginning to thin out some, don't you?"

Marilee brushed at an imaginary blemish on her skirt, her eyes dropping pointedly to Persia's bare toes. Under the barrage of all that sleek, white sharkskin perfection, Persia felt large and untidy and uncomfortably gauche.

Searching desperately for an excuse to remove herself to the far side of the universe, she turned away, and her eyes lighted on the three white-haired women Kathy had introduced as the Snowden sisters. "I'd better see if the Three Graces want anything," she mumbled, hurrying across the cool, damp grass. She fancied she could feel Marsh's eyes boring into her back, and then she derided herself for lapsing into her old failing. Would any normal man be watching a barefooted Amazon in rumpled cotton when he had someone like Marilee clinging to him like Chanel-scented ivy?

Sidetracked by an anguished wail, she located the curly-haired boy whose toy truck had fallen victim to someone's careless foot. "Come on, I know just the man who can fix it for you," she promised recklessly, scooping up child and toy in one sweep and swerving toward where Chip hovered behind the jerry-rigged sound system.

"Chip—dig out your pliers and wire and electrical tape and see what you can do for this driver and his rig."

Leaving the unlikely pair with their heads together over the tool box, she headed for the Misses Snowden. Something about them promised a haven of peace and quiet, and she needed it rather desperately at this point.

"May I bring you some more iced tea?" she offered for openers. "I'm Persia Abernathy. I met you earlier."

"We remember you, dear. You're Kathy's little cousin." Faded blue eyes and guileless persistence swiftly ferreted out the fact that Persia was single, without immediate prospects, and that she was a professional landscaper by trade.

"We never married either, you know," Miss Mary confided.

"Not that we didn't have our followers," Miss Sara put in swiftly.

"Now, girls, Persia doesn't want to hear about our young men. I'm sure she has lots of young men of her own. Tell me." Miss Elizabeth leaned forward confidingly. "Do you think anyone would mind if I took a cutting from that eleagnus? Mine's not nearly as silver."

"I'm sure no one would care at all. It needs pruning, anyway. Shall I get a knife and do it for you?"

A white crocheted bag was recovered from under the lawn chair, and a gnarled hand slipped inside and came out with a lethal-looking switch blade knife. "Use this, dear. I always keep it handy for cuttings. About three short whips, and I'll dip them in talc and set them out under the eaves."

"Miss Elizabeth," Persia blurted, half amused, half horrified, "I think that thing's illegal, isn't it?"

Behind a pair of rimless spectacles, the watery blue eyes blinked uncertainly. "Oh, my goodness, I hope not. My nephew gave it to me when I got so I couldn't open Papa's penknife anymore. It's so handy—perfect for someone with arthritic fingers."

Persia took the cuttings, wrapped them in paper towels, and returned the vicious-looking knife to its unlikely owner. "If these don't do, there's plenty more where they came from. You all just help yourself—I'm sure Tom and Kathy won't mind."

They talked plants for awhile, and Persia was gratefully

aware of the fact that the crowd had dwindled to a dozen or so. Soon now she'd be able to slip away and bury her head under her pillow and cry her eyes out.

"Oh, me, it looks like the party's over," Miss Mary said regretfully. Persia walked them to their elderly Pontiac and waved them off.

Cleanup involved everyone except Marilee, who seemed to be constitutionally exempt from physical labor of any sort. Persia consolidated leftovers without even being tempted, and carried them into the kitchen to find Tom kneeling on the floor with one of Kathy's doll-sized feet in his hand. His look of husbandly concern lifted briefly and he sent Persia a distracted smile.

"Thanks, Persia, honey. The rest of the stuff can wait until tomorrow. I rounded up the paper trash, so nothing will blow."

"What happened?"

"Stubbed her baby toe on one of those old table legs," Tom told her, and Persia wondered how many men, after ten years, would speak of their wife's feet with such ridiculous tenderness.

Feeling uncomfortably like an intruder, she headed for the front porch. She desperately needed some time alone to come to terms with herself before she went upstairs. Wakefulness was bad enough anywhere. In a room that was no more than eight by ten, it took on overtones of claustrophobia.

Ann and Chip were on the loveseat in the living room. Ann's head was on Chip's bony shoulder as they murmured in broken undertones. Without disturbing them, Persia crossed silently to the front door and let herself out. From the screened part of the porch came the creak of the glider and an achingly familiar baritone rumble. Without stopping, she took the steps two at a time.

Before she even reached the pier, the tears had left

crooked trails of silver down her cheeks. Her thin dress was no barrier to the night's cool dampness, and halfway there, she trod on a holly leaf. She swore with fierce emphasis, clutching the misery of self pity to her instinctively as a shield against a much more devastating pain. Gratefully accepting the tepid warmth stored in the satiny old planks, she sank down against the largest piling. As she stared out over the moonlit water of Lake Moultrie, her head back and her eyes wide, she let the tears fall freely. She'd been saving up for hours.

"Oh, you're hopeless—you're a weak, miserable slob," she sniffled, searching for a tissue and for some fragment of self-respect. Today's women were supposed to be above this sort of thing. She hadn't cried when she'd broken her ankle learning to ski. She'd remained stoically dry-eyed when her house had been burgled and she'd lost her father's watch and her mother's pearls. But at times like this, there was no damming the flood.

The sun awakened her, probing her sealed eyes with ruthless fingers. One of these days she'd learn to insist on a westerly exposure. Creaking out of a bed that bore mute testimony to a restless night, she gathered up her working outfit—shorts and a halter that would probably melt at the first touch of perspiration. Mauve handkerchief linen, they'd cost the earth, and she took grim pleasure in wearing them for heavy labor. That should teach her to keep her hands off her credit card when she was in the throes of a fantasy.

Tom and Kathy's door was still closed, as was Chip and Ann's. Marilee's door mocked her silently, and she shut her mind to painful conjecture. If things got too revoltingly pally around her, she'd find some excuse to get out of staying another week.

Breakfast, for once, didn't tempt her. She forced herself

to eat part of a slice of toast and a swallow of milk. Appetites were strange creatures, she acknowledged wryly. After Pat's desertion she'd eaten everything in sight. The visit from his mother had been a one-pound-of-chocolate-covered-cherries occasion, and the time she'd lost the Custis Mall commission by a hair, she'd systematically gone through a whole loaf of oatmeal bread and three quarters of a pound of country butter.

After driving stakes in at the approximate corners, she unwound her ball of twine and set about squaring up the area to be paved. By the time the sun was topping the tallest oak, she had not only established her corners, but she'd laid out the pattern for the center square, the four paths, and the four rectangular flowerbeds. A bit too symmetrical, but given the space limitations, it was the best she could come up with. A sundial would be a nice touch. She'd speak to Tom about it.

The bricks were delivered before she was ready for them, and she ordered them dumped to one side. It was absolute idiocy on her part to have undertaken such a job on the spur of the moment. She'd be exhausted by the time her vacation was over, and she was supposed to start work on the nursing home job as soon as she got back.

So much for Marsh's apprenticeship. She might have known it was all a part of the act. Good buddy Marsh—longtime friend and part-time lover. Until Marilee crooked her manicured pinkie, that is. Persia frowned down at her own grubby nails. She felt the familiar prickling in her eyes and she lifted her face heavenward and swore softly. Only an idiot would fall in love with a man who was obviously already spoken for. If she weren't hurting so damned bad, she'd kick herself!

"Oh, you great big watering pot," she muttered furiously. Sniffling, she began to cut down to a depth of two inches in the areas where the bricks were to go. Cut, scrape, toss. Cut, scrape, toss. She'd have to remind Tom to order a load of sand. She wanted a bed of half an inch, and more to sweep over the finished job to fill the cracks. As the monotony of the hard labor lulled her into a false sense of security, the tears subsided. The security shattered like a crystal unicorn when Marsh called out to her from the back door.

"Better take a break before you fall apart. Brought you some lemonade."

With a vicious swipe, she smeared the combination of tears, perspiration, and dirt across her face. *Oh, God, Persia, you're a real swamp!*

"Thanks," she returned coolly, not looking up from her task. "Leave it on the back steps and I'll get it later."

He was beside her before she had time to gather her defenses. Removing the spade from her hands with quiet forcefulness, he took her elbow and steered her toward the sagging back steps. "Now sit down before you drop," he ordered.

She downed a glassful of the sweet, refreshing liquid and asked for more. "It'll count for the fruit I skipped this morning, in case you're worried."

"I'm worried, all right, but not about your diet," he vowed darkly, studying the flush on her glistening, golden cheeks. "Persia, this is hardly the time or place, but—well, there's something I'd like to talk to you about."

"Oh, are you trying to find an excuse to cancel our bet? Is that why you're plying me with sugary drinks?" Leaning back, she propped her elbows on the step behind her and extended her legs. If he was about to talk to her about the difference between an impulsive pass and a serious, long-term relationship, she'd probably hit him. Meanwhile, she may as well give him an eyeful of what he was going to be missing. Maybe he'd think of her some cold night when he was groping around under the covers for that redheaded bag of bones!

"Damn it, Persia, don't be flippant with me! I don't need this. I've got enough on my mind without having you slam the door in my face every time I try to—"

"You try to what, Marsh? Seduce me? Climb into my bed? I don't recall slamming any doors in your face." She had never sounded breezier. Never mind that she looked like a street cleaner. Never mind that her shorts were stained, her halter sopping wet, her hair a mass of tangles held together with briars and pinestraw. "I really can't imagine what you're complaining about. If you want to unburden yourself and clear your conscience, then why not go find Marilee? Or if she's still on the phone with her Wall Street connection, you could write a letter to Dear Abby." She continued to admire a streak of dirt to the left of her right shinbone as a heavy silence descended over the back steps.

Snapping the match he'd used to light his cigar, Marsh jabbed it into the dirt. For two cents, he'd get the hell out of here and forget he'd ever heard of a woman with the idiotic name of Persia Abernathy. He could have gotten along just fine without this. He'd had it all scheduled; as soon as the bank came through, he'd make it official with Marilee and they'd pick up where they'd left off before, when she'd dropped him cold and run off with a man old enough to be her father. She'd become Mrs. Randolph, and he'd set about forgetting all those bitter years when he'd sworn never to trust another woman.

Instead, he found himself lusting after an unlikely wench with a totally irreverent attitude toward the things most women held dear. A gardener, for Pete's sake! If she had to have a career, why couldn't she have been a secretary, or an interior designer, or any of the other acceptable female occupations? His hazy concept of marriage had been

pretty circumspect, he supposed. A nine-to-five husband
and an attractive wife who played bridge and lunched with
the girls, supported a hairdresser and a couple of dress-
makers, and did a little volunteer work on the side until
the children came.

Kathy, Marilee—they were a type he could deal with.
Up through the ranks of debutante balls and Junior League,
they were the sort of women he'd known all his life. But
how did a man deal with a woman who laughed at the
rain, who laid bricks for the fun of it, and who, according
to what Tom had said, donned a hard hat and tromped
around construction sites laying down the law to a bunch
of bulldozers?

What had come over him since he'd left Columbia? It
was a bit early for the mandatory mid-life crisis. Had he
been pushing himself too hard lately? Was he about to
have a mental breakdown? In the past few days he'd been
asking himself some damned unsettling questions. He'd
thought he'd left those feverish demands of the flesh behind him. If Marilee harbored any similar urgings, it was
news to him. She was probably the most beautiful woman
he'd ever laid eyes on, but as far as the physical urges
were concerned, she simply wasn't all that enthusiastic.

He'd almost accepted the fact that they'd both outgrown
that sort of thing, and then…

This past week had come as a shock to him. He'd come
face to face with a real, live woman whose healthy appetites included all the pleasures, and it had forced him into
some pretty unsettling reevaluations…

He gazed down on the top of her glossy head of tangled
hair and fought a sudden urge to touch it. Could he forget
her after this vacation was over? Could he go back to the
man he'd been and settle down with a faded dream he'd
carried around for so long?

Or did he want a woman who could laugh with him,

play with him, and then welcome him into her bed as if
she really meant it, a woman whose body cradled him as
if he were coming home? Did he want a generous, barefooted woman who took time to fix a child's toy and to
steal cuttings for three sweet-faced old ladies, or did he
want someone who could instantly sum up the net worth
of a social gathering and home in unerringly on any high
rollers.

Once more his eyes were drawn away from the som-
nolent stillness of the oaks to the woman reclining on the
steps below him, and again he felt the sexual restlessness
that came over him with increasing frequency these days.

Revealing a long, delicious expanse between arm and
ankle, Persia leaned back and stretched an arm over her
head to place her glass up on the porch, and Marsh
frowned and shifted his position awkwardly.

"Want to go fishing this afternoon?" he blurted.

Nice going, Randolph. You're already halfway round
the bend—all you need now is to commit yourself to
spending a few more hours alone with this grimy faced
houri, and you'll be throwing away everything you've
wanted for the past dozen years.

His brain was already riddled with visions of Persia in
bed. Sometimes he'd picture her in that clinging nightgown she'd worn the other night, and sometimes she'd be
naked, sprawling abandonedly across the double bed in his
apartment. And then the faceless figure of that damned
Virginia lawyer of hers would intrude, blocking his vision,
and he found himself wanting to strike out viciously at a
man he'd never even met. It was a decidedly irrational
reaction—he hadn't felt anything like it in years.

"Sure. I'll go fishing with you." Her pronouncement,
made in that irritatingly offhand manner, drew forth an
unfriendly scowl. Unfortunately, she missed it entirely.

Pointing her toe and gazing down the rounded length of

her leg, Persia admired the incurve of her ankle. She'd missed nothing. Marsh looked as if he'd regretted his invitation the moment he'd issued it, and she was feeling just wicked enough to hold him to it. These fickle moods of hers—one minute she was in the clouds, the next she was in the pits. They'd just taken another definite upward swing, and she knew intuitively it was because of Marsh's discomfiture. He had something on his mind. It could be—it just possibly *might* be—the fact that he was falling in love with her.

This is your fantasy speaking, a voice intoned inside her head. You'd better know what you're doing, girl. You can break more than your silly little neck tumbling out of castles in the air.

It was delightfully cool out in the middle of the lake. Persia had changed into her bathing suit and the black leghorn picture hat. That hat. Still, it wasn't an utter waste—she could always wear it gardening and fishing.

"Want to swim first, eat first, or fish first?" Marsh asked. Laid back at the controls, he appeared to be almost asleep.

"I'd rather fish later on, when they're hitting the surface. Let's swim now, and then have something to eat. Did you fill the basket, or did Kathy?"

"Would I trust her with your diet?" Marsh asked with mock indignation. "She won't tell me how we're doing on the scales, but I've got a tape measure in the tackle box. Thought I might do a little interim checking, just to be sure everything's under control."

"Unless you're a marlin fisherman, your tape measure won't be up to the job." And if you lay a hand on me, I'll start tearing off your clothes, she simmered silently. With three hundred and sixty degrees of chamber-of-commerce type scenery surrounding them, she couldn't pry her eyes away from him. Fortunately, this time she'd thought to bring her sunglasses.

Marsh cut the motor and they drifted toward the neck of a cove well away from the favored fishing holes. The water, though deep and free of snags, was warmed by the shallower water from the cove. Easing the anchor over the side, he grinned at her. "Can you think of anywhere you'd rather be on a day like this?"

Relinquishing the thought of a highly inappropriate alternative, she shook her head. "How'd you manage to get away without a full boatload?" She unfastened the sari-like coverup that went with her suit and dropped it to the seat as she stepped out of her sandals.

"Tom and Marilee went off somewhere for a quiet huddle about some investments he's considering. Kathy was poring over recipes, and I haven't seen Chip and Ann lately. Maybe they went back to bed."

Marsh slid the ice chest into the shade and stepped out of his khakis. The trunks he was wearing were neither too tight nor too brief, but Persia averted her face and swallowed convulsively. If Dr. Spooner had been here to take her blood pressure now, all his pet theories about weight and health would be validated.

They went over the side and Persia wondered as the cool water closed over her head if she could actually hear a sizzle. She swam underwater for several yards and surfaced well away from where Marsh was treading water. *Down girl! Mustn't covet your neighbor's man.*

In the distance a speedboat passed by, towing two water-skiers. When the wake reached her, Persia floated on her back, enjoying the sensuous motion. Vainly she tried to conquer her erotic thoughts. Cool water caressed her limbs, the sun baked down on the tops of her breasts, and she closed her eyes and sighed. If the whole of Lake Moultrie couldn't cool her off, a paltry cold shower wasn't going to do it, either. This hadn't been a terribly smart move on her part.

From across some five yards of dark, mirrorlike water, Marsh watched her. Her hair drifted out like seaweed, tangling occasionally in her fingers as her hands floated near her head. She was totally relaxed, a state he was finding it harder and harder to come by. From treading water, he rolled over on his back and paddled around so that he could study her between his feet. If only he were the water so that he could cradle her, wrap around her, seep into every part of her body...

And if he didn't watch it, he'd find himself in over his head. He knew a sudden urge to disregard everything in the past and start from here—from now. He'd never reacted to any woman this powerfully—not even in the early days with Marilee.

It had to mean something—but what? If it was merely lust, then why did he seek her company in a houseful of people, where there wasn't the faintest chance of satisfaction of a sexual sort? Why did he feel so protective of her? Why did he feel a genuine craving to discuss with her all the ramifications of the Timmon-Edwards thing, and his ideas of what an independent weekly should and could be? Why did he want to lay bricks with her, to feed her, to laugh with her?

Hell, why did he jump at a chance just to go fishing with her? He'd never fished with a woman before in his life. Marilee wouldn't consider risking her complexion and her manicure, even for a day out in the Gulf Stream aboard an air-conditioned yacht.

He watched as Persia scooped up water and dribbled it over her breasts. Her legs drifted apart and he found his breath quickening. Regardless of what it was he was feeling, he had a hunch it wasn't going to get better until it had got a lot worse. Glancing down at his revealing trunks, he found it expedient to submerge.

"Ouch! I thought you were a snapping turtle," Persia exclaimed a moment later as something nudged her backside. Marsh had drifted up beneath her so that she was lying on his legs, her head resting on his flat stomach.

"Just a friendly alligator," he murmured, his voice sounding strange to her half-submerged ears. His hands reached under her arms and slid her farther on top of him. "Stop struggling—do you want to drown us both?"

"What are you, an air mattress? I don't need any support—Chip says I have built-in buoyancy."

"Yeah, I noticed that Mae West you're wearing."

Flinging an arm over her head, she encountered a nose and twisted. "That's not a Mae West, damn it, it's me!" She was still laughing a moment later as they both sunk beneath the surface.

When they came up again, he waited for her to get her breath, and then he said, "My God, Persia, do you know what you're doing to me?" Turning her to face him, he drew her tightly against him, and she felt her legs entangle with his. "It's hardly something I can keep secret, under the circumstances. What are we going to do about it?"

With a sledgehammer pounding at her ribs and her heart lodged somewhere in her throat, she whispered, "What do you want to do about it?"

He moved his hips against her and groaned. "You have to ask?" Staring intensely into her eyes, he raked the straps of her suit down over her arms and lifted her hands free. As the scrap of coral swirled slowly down around her waist, he swayed lightly from side to side, brushing the wet curls on his chest over her erect nipples.

"Marsh, your sense of timing is dreadful," she said shakily.

Supporting her with his hands, he lowered himself in

the water and buried his face in the creamy valley between her glistening breasts. "You don't know the half of it, precious," he groaned. "I was all set to get myself engaged to Marilee. I've bought the ring and I suspect she knows it—and I think I'm falling in love with you. I can't figure out any other possible explanation for the way I'm feeling."

She shut her eyes against the unbelievable sweetness of it. It couldn't be true—she must be still fantasizing. Slithering swiftly through his hands, she brought her mouth on a level with his and pleaded wordlessly with him. When the long, searching kiss ended, she drew away just enough to see his face, his dear, familiar, wet face. "Marsh, do you have any idea at all just how long I've loved you?"

"Oh, sweetheart, don't tell me that," he protested, tucking her face into his neck and stroking her from her head to the lower curve of her back.

Her legs had a tendency to drift upward, and she let them go. They wound around his hips, and she hugged him fiercely. "You don't want me to love you?" A sliver of doubt crept in; it had been too good to be true. She'd only imagined the words he'd said.

With her body clinging to his, Marsh began to paddle them to the far side of the boat, where they were hidden between the aluminum hull and the densely wooded bank. "I'm just selfish enough to want it more then anything in the world, but it's not fair to you. Or to the other two people involved."

"There's only one, but if you love me and I love you, then that's more important than anything, isn't it?" *Please, please,* she prayed, *don't take this away from me. Not now—not when it's almost within my grasp.*

Hidden from the occasional passing boat, Marsh allowed his hands to slide under the bottom half of her suit and ease it down over her legs. Words—reason—all that could come later. For now, there was something else he had to do. "Don't lose your suit," he warned, then dived under to catch the silky shred of fabric as it drifted downward, and his eyes lingered on the pale, wavery image before him as he surfaced again. With the fleeting vision etched indelibly on his mind, he tossed the suit into the boat and removed his own.

Slowly, as if every move had been choreographed as a water ballet, Marsh lowered himself beneath the surface once more. While Persia hung suspended before him, her toes pointing downward and her arms moving only enough to maintain her balance, he swam down and brushed his lips over the arch of her feet. Then, drifting slowly upward, he tasted the cool surface of her knees and slid his mouth up the graceful columns of her thighs, savoring the heat that lay just beneath the skin. As the pressure in his lungs increased, he brushed lingering kisses over the patch of sensuous darkness, thrilling as she trembled at his touch. And then he moved on to the tiny indentation that centered the delicious swell of her belly.

He darted a tongue into the shallow depression, delighting as her back arched and her legs stiffened. Swiftly, he surfaced between her breasts and caught her to him. "God, you're marvelous!" he panted. "You make me wish I were a fish."

"I'm so glad you're not," she gasped huskily as she adjusted herself to the fascinating contours of his masculine body. Sometime—next time—she'd favor him with a leisurely underwater exploration, but for now, it was all she could do to keep from drowning as he tantalized each demanding nipple with a hot, caressing tongue.

Finally, when she was frenzied with need, he drew her to him. This time when her legs drifted up and around his hips, he cupped a hand under her and adjusted her position.

"I'm not sure this is going to work," he rasped. The planes of his face were flattened harshly.

And then it did. With a sound that was part sigh, part sob, she gasped his name.

"Oh, love, don't move—don't even breathe, or I won't be able to stop."

They hung suspended there, and Persia wondered in the dim recesses of her mind if the very hammering of their pulses would spread a warm wake from shore to shore.

"I love you, Marsh. I love—ooooh," she sighed as he began to move.

She knew she didn't have enough strength left in her to climb back aboard the float boat. "Are you sure you can't throw me a line and tow me behind the boat?"

"Honey, if I ever trolled with bait like you, I'd have every fisherman on the lake snapping after us."

They were drifting lethargically on their backs, fingers entwined and feet hooked together. Sooner or later they had to talk; there were still too many unsettled issues between them. But not now. For now she wanted to hold the knowledge of his love inside her as long as possible. It was too new to share, too precious to risk.

"There's no one in sight at the moment," Marsh said drowsily. "I'll climb up and give you a hand. I reckon we'd better put on a few clothes."

"Couldn't we stay just a little longer?" It wasn't that she was afraid of returning to the others, it was just that...

She *was* afraid of returning to the others. It would be awkward at the very least. Where did Kathy's loyalty lie? With her cousin, or with her best friend? Could they all manage to spend the next week under the same roof, or was this going to spell an end to the Gaillards' tenth anniversary house party?

"There's food aboard if you're open to bribery."

"Wretch. I'm starving. Go first and drop my suit over the side. I'm not about to climb into that boat jaybird naked in broad daylight."

Righting himself in the water, Marsh clasped each side of her face and kissed her. As she jostled gently against his body, her lips clinging to his sweet, savory mouth, her hands came up over to flatten on his chest, and her fingertips found the small brown circles of his nipples.

He groaned against her mouth. "Oh, sweetheart, don't tempt me. Not so soon—not in this cold water. Behave yourself." He bit her chin gently and nuzzled the curve of her throat, bringing a rush of goosebumps down her side.

Reluctantly she let him go, and then she watched unashamedly as he eased himself over the side. Sunlight glistened on his tanned shoulders, on the dark, crisply curled hair that patterned his torso. Everything about him was beautiful, and she felt a swift rise of misgivings about her own body. Under the water she'd felt safe—in a darkened bedroom, she'd feel secure enough in her nudity, but out here in the middle of the lake, with the sun shining mercilessly down on her?

Marsh held up her suit. "I don't think you're going to be able to get into this thing without a lot of trouble. Let me hold up the thingamajig you wore over it and screen you while you come aboard. There's no one close by."

"I'll manage," she said adamantly. He'd seen her in all those cleverly styled clothes, and under a distorting lens of water. She wasn't about to gamble everything she'd just won by exhibiting herself to someone who was used to a slender little size eight. "Just pass it over and go fix lunch, will you?"

He insisted on watching her while she twisted about, struggling to tug a tight wet suit on over cold wet flesh. It wasn't easy. "Do you have to stand there gawking?"

"Yep."

She ducked under and managed to get her feet through the proper holes, and then she wrestled the suit up over her body. The straps twisted painfully and cut into her shoulders, but she finally covered herself enough to climb aboard with a remnant of modesty. "Voyeur," she charged, dripping all over his dry khakis.

"Yep."

"Is that all you can say? Don't answer!" Padding across to where she'd left her towel, she dried herself enough to drape the sarong around her waist. "Now, will you please feed me?" she demanded, parking herself on the shady side of the boat. She gazed up at the lean figure silhouetted against the sun-struck canopy. "Picnics don't count on the diet—I hope you remembered that."

He poured two glasses of wine and then he sat down beside her and reached into the basket. "Try one of these," he offered, holding a finger sandwich filled with something sinfully delectable. "Just your basic cream cheese, capers and anchovies. D'you like those sausage and cheese things Kathy baked?" He held out a small roll and she bit off half of it. He popped the rest into his mouth and smiled beatifically.

"Marsh, we have to talk," she mumbled after she'd devoured the sausage roll. She washed it down with a swallow of chilled chablis.

"Here—special treat for registered professional mermaids." He held out a cookie, rich with dark rum and coconut and pecans. She bit into it and he ate the rest of it and reached into the basket once more.

"Marsh, what are you trying to do to me? Please—we have to talk. At least, I have to tell you about Patrick." She broke off as he offered her a small cracker spread with a mixture of ham, chutney and thick cream, topped with shredded cheese. "Marsh, where are you getting all this food? Kathy didn't have any of these things yesterday. Are you trying to buy my silence?" Resignedly, she took a bite of the latest treat and then leaned back against the railing. "How can you do this to me? Does it make you happy to search out my every weakness and exploit it?"

"Yep." Calmly, he topped off her wineglass. She lifted it, drained it, and then glared at him.

"Don't start that Gary Cooper thing again! Marsh, I'm going to tell you about Patrick whether you want to listen or not! And then if you want to tell me anything in return, well—well, feel free," she ended lamely as the short burst of belligerence left her.

Chapter Nine

I only want to know one thing about your Virginian," Marsh said flatly. "Do you love him?"

"Well, of course I don't love him," Persia explained patiently. "I love you."

"Then what was between the two of you?"

"I thought you only wanted to know one thing." Persia leaned back against the railing, a feeling of unease slipping under her guard as Marsh prepared to get underway.

"Make it two. What were you to Patrick? His friend? His lover? Did the two of you live together?"

"His fiancée, and no we did not live together. I happen to own my own house, and it's hardly the sort of place Patrick would be comfortable in. He lives with his mother and sister at Hickory Oaks Farms." She'd been the one to insist on putting all the cards on the table. It was a bit late for second thoughts.

"He's a farmer, too? Is that what the attraction was?"

"No, he's not a farmer. If you must know, it's a tax farm," she snapped. She hadn't known that until shortly before they'd broken up.

"So what happened?" He lifted the anchor aboard and started the motor, steering them out of the cove. The sun had already sunk below the tops of the distant trees, leaving a hazy stillness hovering just above the water.

"He broke it off."

His eyes narrowed. "*He* broke it off? Is he deranged? Mentally incompetent?"

"Marsh, if you want me to answer your questions seriously, then stop being so—so—" She shrugged helplessly. From euphoria, she'd been plunged directly into uncertainty, and it was growing by the minute.

"When did you break up? How long were you engaged?"

"What difference could that possibly make? We were engaged for five months, and we broke up a couple of months ago. That's not important now. The point is, I..."

The point was, she'd been in love with them both. Before, during, and after Patrick, there had been Marsh. He'd been a subliminal factor in her life since she was sixteen. "I roomed with Pat's sister, Megan, at college. She lived on campus even though the farm's only twenty miles or so from Fredericksburg—to get away from her mother, I think. I met Pat the first time I went home with Megan for holidays. He was handsome, debonair, courtly—all those fancy words they use in fairy tales. But most of all, he was kind. I was a lot heavier then, but Pat didn't care. I wasn't all that experienced with men, either, but it didn't seem to bother him."

Marsh's face took on a look of grimness and he adjusted the throttle for maximum speed. "Damned big of him, I must say! So he was kind. And handsome, and debonair, and courtly," he jeered.

Confused by his sudden inexplicable shift of moods, Persia covered her uncertainty with aggressiveness. She jammed the leghorn hat on her wet head and tilted her chin arrogantly. "Yes, he was. Furthermore, he still is. And it was Patrick who took me home when Daddy died and helped me straighten out the mess about the state, and I was only his sister's roommate back then. He handled the sale of the house, and arranged with the trustee for my tuition, and I didn't even have to meet any of Daddy's creditors. He wouldn't take a penny for his services, either. And then, last Christmas, he asked me to marry him."

"Bully for our courtly hero."

"Marsh, what's the matter with you?" She bit her lip, searching for a clue to what had brought on this sudden coolness between them. Surely he couldn't be jealous. Not of Patrick. "I thought we—well, you said you loved me."

Correction; he'd said he *thought* he *might* be falling in love with her. That was a process, not a condition.

He cut the motor. In the sudden ringing silence, he stood up and moved swiftly toward her. Before they'd even lost momentum, he was apologizing. "Persia, I'm sorry, honey. Believe me, I don't want to hurt you. It's just that I—well, in case you hadn't noticed, I'm *not* the courtly, debonair type, and damn it, I'm messing this all up before I even get it off the ground." He looked so abject, so acutely uncomfortable, that Persia wanted to gather him to her and comfort him.

Lifting her hands impulsively, she allowed them to fall again. She felt as if she were walking on eggshells; one false step and something incredibly beautiful and fragile would be crushed beyond restoring. "Marsh, please be patient with me. I told you—I'm not very experienced at this sort of thing, but I do love you." She waited for his declaration, her courage seeping away with every moment's silence.

"Persia, when it comes to experience, I'm not much better off than you are. I fell for Marilee so long ago I didn't really have time to get involved with other women. We saw each other every weekend for almost four years, mostly with Tom and Kathy. Then, after I got established to the point where I could afford a wife, I bought a ring and memorized a speech. Before I could propose, she'd gone to Chicago with Kurtz, and the next thing I heard was that she'd married him."

This time her hands came up and rested on his shoulders. "Oh, Marsh, I'm so sorry," she murmured. Sorry? What was she saying?

"So you see, what with carrying a torch for several years, and then a lot of bitterness that kept me from getting close to any other women, I'm a novice at this sort of thing."

"When did you start seeing her again?"

"After she moved back to Columbia, we had lunch a few times. I guess I was still pretty gun-shy. Oh, there were several women in between, but nothing important. I didn't see Marilee again until the divorce was final."

Persia tried to pretend that it didn't matter now—all those years of loving Marilee, all the other women he must have made love to. She'd dated all through school, too, and there'd been Patrick. But that was different.

"She's as beautiful as ever. I guess that was what attracted me in the first place, and I didn't have sense enough to want something more. Childish, huh?"

"But very human," she said softly, loving him, knowing how it must have hurt his pride to be thrown aside for a man old enough to be his father.

"Which brings us full circle. I made up my mind that if I was ever going to have a family and a home, other than the inefficiency apartment I've lived in since Dad remarried, it was time to make my move. So—last month I bought a ring. I figured I'd pick a romantic spot, throw in a little moonlight and music, and ask her.'' His eyes roved over her face, lingering on her mouth and then returning to her softly glistening eyes. ''And then you showed up.''

She waited. And then he fell head over heels in love with her? And then he realized that he could never be truly happy without her? ''Well?'' she prompted as her expectations continued to go unfilled. *''Well?''*

A bass boat passed, and two fishermen waved and called out, ''Had any luck?''

Persia's hands dropped from Marsh's shoulders and she drew in a deep, shaky breath. Inexperienced she might be, but she knew when it was time to back off. The next move was his.

''I hope they're not expecting to have our catch for dinner tonight. As a fishing team, we don't have a very outstanding record.'' She laughed shakily as she turned away and reached for her sunglasses. So what if the sun had already set? She wasn't above a touch of affectation when the occasion demanded. The way he'd been probing her eyes, none of her secrets would be safe with him, and until things were a lot further along than this, she didn't care to reveal all those years of hopeless longing. She'd been dumped once and so had he. Maybe they'd both be better off for taking it slow and easy.

Only she wasn't a slow-and-easy type, she acknowledged in silent misery as they drew alongside the pier several minutes later. She was an all-or-nothing type. Any appearance of rectitude and stoicism she'd developed over the years was only skin deep.

She leaped out and took the lines, and Marsh tended to the motor and handed out their unused tackle and the empty lunch basket. Face it, she told herself as she stared out across the somber lake; for all her practicality, she was a hopeless optimist, a daydreamer, an unrepentant romantic who couldn't keep her heart's secret if her life depended on it. So she'd blurted it all out. And Marsh had gone all funny and guarded. As a result, she'd grown wary, and now they were ricocheting off each other like bullets in a cheap Western.

"It's about time you two showed up." Tom was waiting on the porch as they trudged up the walk. They'd been out longer than she'd realized. Persia felt as if she could sleep for a year. She was waterlogged—exhausted both mentally and physically.

"What's up?" Marsh called out softly through the thick amber dusk that hung heavily over the narrow, wooded peninsula.

"Your secretary called twice. She wants you to call her at home." As Marsh swore softly under his breath, Tom turned to Persia, his good-natured features taking on an uncharacteristic dourness. "You had a call, too. Didn't leave a number—said he'd try again when he got a chance."

In the kitchen Persia shook out the napkin that lined the basket, tossed it into the laundry hamper, and put the nearly empty wine bottle in the refrigerator. Who on earth could it have been? Her boss? It had to be—he was the only one who knew where she was. Normally she'd have told Megan Blake, but things had been a bit awkward between them since the breakup.

Showering and dressing, she allowed her mind to explore the possibilities. It weren't as if Shamburg Landscaping, Inc., hadn't muddled along without her for thirty-seven years. Surely they could manage without her services for two weeks out of the year.

The board of directors must have thrown a wrench in the plans she'd done for the nursing home. Totally conservative, they'd wanted the grounds to be as traditional and as formal as the interior of the enormous old Georgian building. But the managing director had agreed with her idea for converting most of the back into an easy-care plot where the "guests" could raise whatever vegetables took their fancy with little work at all. She'd explained that a heavy mulch and a monthly visit from someone from the shop would be all that was necessary. It was her private theory that once it got established, the residents, wealthy and elderly for the most part, would catch gardening fever and take over the complete care of the plot. The exercise, not to mention the interest, would be marvelous therapy.

Of course, there was always someone around to remind her that she was a landscape architect and not an expert on geriatrics. But after her experience in designing a playground for a day-care center, complete with espaliered trees that would one day become living playthings, she'd dared to offer an innovative plan.

The dinner Kathy had worked so hard over was faultlessly prepared, but no one seemed to have an appetite. Chip and Ann were wrapped up in each other. He'd had a hair cut and she was wearing a new green polo shirt, and while it didn't bring about any miraculous transformation, it was a step in the right direction. Tom had surprisingly little to say about Marsh's empty stringer. He excused himself halfway through the meal to fly-fish along the bank before it grew too dark.

"Marilee, have some gumbo. You missed it the first go around." Kathy's expression began to look dismayed as her food continued to go unappreciated. As one after another of the house guests refused, Persia took the bowl and helped herself. It wasn't fair for people to take out their troubles on poor Kathy, who'd spent all afternoon working on the gumbo, stuffed guinea squash, corn pie and chicken fricassee.

"What about your diet?" Kathy protested.

"Stuff the diet," Persia retorted inelegantly. "Why

should I be miserable just because everyone else is?'' She forked up a bite of chicken, mentally running over the list of ingredients from force of habit and finding it relatively harmless.

Marilee toyed with a slice of the delectabley stuffed egg-plant while she told Marsh about the latest drop in interest rates, which, if it were indicative of a trend, might mean a sale for her house within the next month or so.

Persia picked out a large bit of bacon from the rice dish and scowled at it. She waited for some indication from Marsh that he was less than fascinated by Marilee's finan-cial wheelings and dealings.

''That's nice, honey,'' he muttered, salting his un-touched meal for the second time.

''Nice! Marsh, do you realize what it means? If I'm stuck in the middle of negotiating a sale for the house, then I won't be able to use it as collateral, and by the time—''

There was more, but Persia tuned it out. She poked mo-rosely at the buttery corn pie, and as soon as she decently could, she excused herself from the table. ''Leave things right here, Kath—I'll be back to take care of it.'' She avoided Marsh's searching gaze as she hurried out the back door.

Pacing the perimeters of the shallow excavation in the backyard, she strained to hear the low murmur of voices from inside. Surely they'd be finished soon. Marsh could make some excuse and join her out here. In fact she could wait on the bench. He'd guess where she was. She might even up-end it and show him the pair of initials she'd whittled out so long ago. That should convince him if he still needed convincing.

By the time it had grown completely dark, she was al-most nauseated from tension and disappointment. If he'd been going to join her, he'd have been here by now.

Maybe it required more time than she'd thought to break off a relationship—if that's what he was doing. All she had to go by was her own experience. Patrick had sent in an advance party to soften her up, so that by the time he came to deliver the coup de grace, it was all over but the shouting.

She sighed. Then she swore softly. If there was one thing she abhorred, it was sighing, crying females, and just lately she'd been both. And she couldn't blame starvation, either. Diet or no diet, in the short time she'd been here, she'd managed to put away enough forbidden treats to last her a year. Her fingers stroked the rough surface of the ancient bench, and then they curled under the edge, feeling in the darkness for a certain pattern.

She yelped and jerked her hand back, cramming her finger into her mouth. A snakebite? She hardly thought so. In the split second before the pain slammed down on her forefinger, she'd felt the familiar shape of a paper wasp's construction.

"So now go on and bawl," she grumbled aloud. "At least you've got an excuse."

They were still talking out there on the porch by the time she'd got herself ready for bed. When she'd finally wandered back to the house, the table had been waiting for her. Someone had put away the food, and she'd lingered over the task of rinsing the dishes and stacking them in the dishwasher. She hated the noise, but at least it served to block out the murmur of voices coming from the screened porch.

Chip and Ann had turned in embarrassingly early, and Tom had chewed on his pipe stem and worked on a handful of battered old lures. Kathy had curled up on the sofa with a magazine, so that left Marsh and Marilee. How long did it take a man to tell a woman it was all off?

Shortly after ten, Persia gave up and went upstairs.

Through her open window, a whipoorwill taunted her over the soft mumble of voices from the screened porch. He's being tactful, she told herself. After all, their relationship went back at least a dozen years. You didn't just end something like that in five minutes.

She lay awake and stared at the ceiling, caressing the knobby footboard with the sole of her foot. Surely he'd come upstairs soon. In all decency, he'd probably have to wait until Marilee was safely tucked away. It would hardly be tactful to come upstairs with his old love, bid her good night, and then let himself into his new love's bedroom.

She got up and peeled her nightgown over her head and then climbed back in bed, arranging the sheet to cover all but the top of her breasts. She'd brushed her hair and wafted the perfume atomizer in the air, and then walked through the fragrant mist. Subtlety; she was learning. She'd brushed her teeth, rinsed with mouthwash, and lotioned herself all over. Then she'd dabbed a hint of color on her lips and cheeks. Not enough to smear—just enough to enhance.

Was nudity subtle? Hardly! She leaped out of bed again and felt for her gown. A little mystery was supposed to be more arousing, wasn't it? And in case he was inclined to put on his reading glasses and take a flashlight to search for stretch marks, she didn't have to make it easy for him. She had a few. Marsh had probably never even seen one before. Women like Marilee wouldn't recognize a stretch mark if they tripped over it in broad daylight. Could she convince him that the tiny silvery trails on the sides of her hips were scars from some dramatic life-or-death operation? What important organ could be reached through the hips?

She sighed again, swallowed a lump in her throat and chewed off her lipstick. Then she fell asleep.

* * *

For several minutes he stood in the doorway and gazed at the form under the sheet. He could barely make out the dark shadow of her hair as it flowed across the pillow. Should he awaken her? He was going to have to get an early start if he intended to meet Ridings at the bank at nine.

He was exhausted, though. Today had been...

Remembering, he smiled and closed the door silently. Today had been the most important day of his life. The whole of his existence would pivot on what had happened this afternoon, but before he could proceed, he had some old business to clear up. He'd been brought up to believe that a gentleman didn't play off one woman against another. If that was an outdated code—and it probably was— then he'd still have to risk it. This thing with Persia was far too important to mishandle any single aspect of it. He'd have to "off with the old" before he dared "on with the new." Once he committed himself, he wanted no untidy ends from the past to trip him up.

Lying in the single bed Chip had traded for the double upstairs, he searched his mind for the easiest way to break off with Marilee. It was just his rotten luck that the owner of the jewelry store where he'd bought her ring had more mouth than he had judgment. She'd known about it since the day after he'd picked it up. Before he'd even been able to steer the subject around to Persia tonight, she'd asked if he minded if she traded it in on a sapphire. While she appreciated the thought of his trying to find a stone to match her eyes, emeralds were just too soft to be practical. They'd been known to fracture for no reason at all.

The call tonight had been both fortunate and unfortunate. He was going to have to go back to Columbia, and possibly to Knoxville, as well. Which was a good excuse to get Marilee away from here. On the other hand, he didn't like rushing off without having a chance to talk to

Persia. He'd probably made a mess of things today. The whole thing had come down on him like a ton of bricks—the restlessness he'd been feeling, this fascination with every word she uttered, every move she made, the urge to strike out at that damned lawyer of hers. Jealousy. Pure and simple. And if he was that jealous, then it stood to reason that he cared for her a hell of a lot more than he'd realized.

He'd known this afternoon. As soon as he'd made love to her—oh, sweet heaven, had anything ever been so perfect?—he'd realized what had happened to him, why he'd been so numb where Marilee was concerned.

But it didn't make sense. He'd known Persia for a single week. He'd been in love with Marilee practically all his life—at least he'd thought it was love. Now he was beginning to wonder if he'd ever even known her. Under that flawless facade she had all the warmth of a cash register, and part of what made him so damned furious with himself now was the fact that he'd wasted all these years waiting for a woman who didn't even exist.

Tomorrow, and all the tomorrows after that, he'd make up for it. His eyes closed and he groaned softly as his anxious thoughts flattened out and slid away.

"But why didn't you wake me up?" Persia wailed. Kathy had been sitting at the table nursing a cup of coffee while she finished a novelette in her magazine.

"Why should I wake you up? They just went home for a day or so. Even if Marsh gets tied up longer, Marilee will probably come back without him."

In a pig's eye! Whatever excuse they'd come up with, Persia was in no mood to be placated. She poured herself a cup of coffee, dosed it with cream and sugar, and then helped herself to a toasted muffin. Slathering it with butter and apricot jam, she struggled to hide her dismay. Marsh and Marilee had left only minutes ago. She'd been in the shower shampooing, and then she'd borrowed Kathy's blowdryer so that her hair would be all gleaming highlights this morning.

"Looks like your house party's coming apart at the seams," she mumbled around her muffin. Was he trying to tell her something? Was he already regretting yesterday?

"I guess two weeks was too much to shoot for. One might have been better." Kathy wrinkled her nose and sighed. "Chip and Ann are leaving either today or tomorrow, too. Chip promised they'd be back for Saturday night. I mean, Tom bought all those tickets, and then when Ann showed up, he managed to wangle one more."

"I'm sure Marsh and Marilee won't forget. They'll be back, and you all can all squeeze in one car. I think maybe I'd better shove off a few days early."

"Per-sia," Kathy wailed. "Don't you dare! I haven't seen you since Uncle Madison died, and if you run back up north again, it will be ages!"

"Up north? Kathy, do you have any real conception of just where the Commonwealth of Virginia is located?"

"North of here."

Persia's personal dark cloud split to allow a smile to shine through. "Score one for the home team. But honestly, Kath, it wouldn't be a bad idea for me to clear out of here. I don't think I can take much more of your cooking without bursting out of everything I brought to wear."

And if Marsh comes back with that woman, I think I'll curl up and die!

Kathy's lower lip jutted threateningly. "You mean you're just going to dig up our whole backyard and then walk out and leave it?"

Oh, Lord, she'd forgotten that. Unconsciously, she reached for another muffin and piled on butter and jam. She stared at it, and then she placed it on her cousin's plate and turned her back on temptation. "Okay, I'll stay. But as soon as I finish the patio, I really will have to head back to Virginia."

"Persia, have you had another fight with Marsh?"

Persia took back her muffin and bit into it. Chewing, she shook her head emphatically. "Better get at it before it gets too hot," she mumbled, swallowing the last of her coffee and hurrying to the back door.

How could anyone be so dense? Kathy wasn't known for her intellect, but how could *anyone* be oblivious to something so—so earth-shaking? Had Tom guessed? Chip had certainly picked up on it quickly enough.

Persia dusted her hands on the seat of her shorts and reached for the rake. While she smoothed out the footprints from the bed of sand, she fought to keep the doubts from closing over her head. Marsh wouldn't make love to her and then pretend it had never happened. He wasn't like that.

How do you know what he's like? All you have to go by is a brief contact ten years ago, a batch of dog-eared wedding pictures, and a few days shared with a houseful of other people, including Marilee. He could be a yellow-headed Bluebeard for all you know.

She confronted her devil's advocate squarely. He told you he loved you.

Ah, she argued, but how many men would say that under similar circumstances? Besides, he hadn't exactly said he loved her. He'd said he *thought* he was *falling* in love with her. Maybe he'd been mistaken. Maybe he'd had second thoughts. Maybe she'd better concentrate on what she was doing before she scratched her way to China!

The sun filtered through the trees with increasing ferocity as Persia worked her pattern of bricks from the center outward. She'd planned originally to lay herself a platform of planks to work from, but now she wanted only to finish the project and get away. He'd probably arranged for his secretary to call him so he'd have an excuse to escape an embarrassing situation. So she'd lay these blasted bricks and pack her bags and get out of here, and then Tom could give the all clear signal, and the house party could go it's merry, blissful, two-by-two way!

"You're awfully quiet," Marilee observed as they pulled away from a service station just north of Santee. "Afraid your little playmate won't wait for you?"

Marsh winced. He'd been expecting something of this sort ever since they'd left Pinopolis. Marilee had been entirely too cheerful, too willing to accommodate herself to his early schedule. It wasn't like her to accommodate herself to anything outside her own interests.

"I take it you're referring to Persia?" At least he wouldn't have to waste any more time trying to be tactful. Damn it, if she'd known all along, why had she put him through all that business last night? Once she'd started reminiscing about their early days, he hadn't been able to shut her up. He should have known she was up to something. Beautiful she may be; smart she undoubtedly was, but Marilee didn't have a sentimental bone in her body. Never had—never would.

"How long have you known?"

"Longer than you have, probably." She leaned over to smooth the calf of her nylons, slanting him a feline smile under the smooth curtain of hair. "You always were a fool, Marsh. I knew the minute you fell in love with me, and the minute you started panting after her. You're hopelessly transparent, darling."

"You're probably right." He nodded, quietly furious. "What puzzles me though, is why you put up with it. You knew I'd planned to propose to you. Why didn't you interfere if you thought I was straying?"

"Why should I? Darling, you don't think I'm worried about someone like Persia Abernathy, do you? I'm not the jealous sort. It's a waste of energy. I knew you'd get it out of your system one way or another and come back where you belonged. I take it you two had sex yesterday afternoon?"

Marsh felt the heat rise to his face. His knuckles whitened on the steering wheel and he waited until he could control his temper to speak. God, to think he'd ever thought he loved her! She said the word as if it were something disgusting. "I don't think it's any of your business, Marilee. Last night I tried to tell you—"

"I know you did," she purred sweetly.

"If you knew, why all the pretense?"

"Darling, I'm not stupid. I know you better than anyone. I know where your weak spots are, and I know how to use them. You're tough-looking on the outside, but inside, you're a marshmallow."

The knuckles went from white to red as his eyebrows came down heavily. "Go on—I'm fascinated by your insight."

"That's what makes it so perfect," she declared, turning on the seat so that she faced him. "To look at me, no man would think I have a gray cell in my head, but you and I know that's not true. Freddie saw right through my beauty to the real me. That's what fascinated him so. I almost wish he'd adopted me instead of marrying me—then I wouldn't have had to leave him."

"You know, you're incredible. What made you divorce the man if he was so damned perfect?" If he hadn't been so thunderously angry, he'd have been amused; whatever she was, there couldn't be many more like her. It was a good thing he'd come to his senses in time.

"He kept clearing his throat."

It took him a moment. "He kept—? You mean you divorced your husband because he cleared his throat?"

"You don't understand—he cleared his throat constantly. I think it was a sort of nervous habit or something. Anyway, I couldn't take it. It's no fun being married to an old man, even one as powerful as Freddie. We're still friends. I'm like a daughter to him."

Marsh let her talk. Nothing she said now could possibly affect him, but he had to get through the drive to Columbia. Eyes grim with purpose, he pressed the accelerator and forced himself to relax.

"My father never had any use for me," Marilee continued—she'd been talking relentlessly, but he'd tuned out most of it. "He wanted a son to take over his affairs, and all he got was a little carrot-topped runt of a daughter. Did you know that all he left me was a trust fund? He left the business outright to my cousin Ned. And I wish to hell he was alive now so that he could see what that poor fool's done with his precious corporation!"

From the corner of his eye, Marsh saw the small, flawlessly manicured hands knot into fists. "I spent years thinking of how I was going to get my hands on enough voting stock to drive it into the ground, and Neddie beat me to it, damn him."

He felt sick. He felt sorry for her—it was like seeing someone unmasked, and it was no pleasure at all. "Why me? I've never been in the same league as Kurtz or your father."

"I thought you were. I always took it for granted you had your father's money and position behind you," she said candidly. "But it wasn't all that important. Forget Persia—she'll never amount to anything, but you and I would make an unbeatable team. There are still a few places where a man can be more effective than a woman, and with your background and personality and my looks and brains, we'd be terrific. Did you know that Freddie's promised to get me a seat on his board of directors? And Freddie's over sixty years old and he has emphysema.''

Marsh swallowed the nausea that burned his throat. He couldn't take any more of it. He'd actually thought he had to let her down gently. God, what a blind fool he was! All he wanted to do now was to dump her out of the car, get through with his business, and get back to Persia.

He reached out and pushed in a tape. When the strains of Schmidt's Fourth Symphony filled the car, Marilee gave him a curious look, but she didn't speak again until they were on the outskirts of town.

"Will you be back after your meeting at the bank?"

He didn't pretend to misunderstand. "I don't think so." He turned off the Interstate and took Klapman Boulevard to Forest Drive. Odd that they'd both grown up in the same section of town, yet they'd never met until he was in college. He'd been off at Hampton-Sydney while Marilee finished high school at home, and then she'd gone on to Sweetbriar. Marsh had worked for a year or two on the *Constitutional,* and then entered U.S.C. with some idea of getting into textile engineering. His father's financial responsibilities had increased with his remarriage and John Paul's birth, and Marsh had wanted to be within reach if he were needed.

"You're really being foolish about this, you know," Marilee said as they pulled up in front of her house. "You're going to throw yourself away on a woman who won't be a bit of good to you when it comes to getting ahead. Her father ruined himself before he died, and Persia—she's nice enough, but that won't be enough for a man like you, Marsh. You're too strong—that's what attracted me to you in the first place—that quiet, understated strength of yours.''

Marsh managed a wintery smile. "I wouldn't expect you to understand, Marilee. And now, if you'll excuse me?"

When the door closed behind her, he sat quietly for several moments, conscious of a feeling of emptiness. And then, as the void began to fill with a warm, sweet expectancy, a smile flickered to life and spread across his face. If he'd worn a hat he'd probably have tossed it into the air.

Ridings, the bank manager, was unusually cheerful. Marsh fidgeted while he discussed a new rule at the country club affecting the use of golf carts. He appended his signature to the bottom of several sheets of fine print and asked about Mrs. Ridings. By nine-twenty he was finished. He could be back in Pinopolis by early afternoon if all went well.

All did not go well. His secretary met him at the door of his cluttered office with the news that his managing editor adamantly refused to go to Knoxville and was considering a bid from the *Charlotte Observer*. A whole page of ads had been inadvertently left out of one edition, and his most reliable copy editor was out sick.

"Persia if you don't get up off your knees and get inside this house, I'm going to squirt the hose on you," Kathy called from the back porch.

"Wonderful! Wait until it runs cold first, though, will you?" Persia extended one leg to see if her knee still worked. "I should have worn long pants, I guess."

"You guess! Honey, I didn't mean that you should finish the whole patio today," Kathy admonished. "I just wanted an excuse to keep you from running off before your vacation was over."

Clamping a hand to her back, Persia managed to stand upright without swaying too much. Her knees felt as if sand had worked into the very joints, and her eyes were stinging from perspiration. "Fat chance. I won't be able to bend myself under the wheel of my car for a week. Why didn't you send Tom out to help me? I plopped one brick in the center of the square, and then there was no turning back. It's compulsive—like peanuts or potato chips."

Kathy held the door open and waited until Persia had dusted off the worst of the sand. "Believe me, you wouldn't want Tom around. I don't know what's got into that man. He's been stomping around here like a bear with a sore head ever since Marsh and Marilee got off this morning. He hardly even told them good-bye."

"I'd better shower off before I sit down at the table. The board of health might shut down your kitchen if I walked in looking like this."

Standing under a stream of lukewarm water, Persia felt it all coming back. For hours now she'd been able to shut out all the doubts, all the painful uncertainty. Butting one brick against another, fitting them together in the design she'd worked out, and squashing them into the sand, she'd been able to close her mind to Marsh and Marilee.

Where were they now? Were they together? In Marilee's house? In Marsh's apartment? She flung the sponge down and stuck her head under the water again, taking perverse pleasure in the pain of shampoo in her eyes. At least she was cured of her fantasy. It was no one-dimensional paper hero she was aching for now, but a real live flesh-and-blood man, a man with hands that could set alight every cell in her body and lips that could fuel the flames.

She'd give him until tomorrow. If she hadn't heard from him by then, she'd take off. And if he showed up again with Marilee, she'd die first, and then she'd leave.

Chapter Ten

"Persia? You awake?" Kathy touched a burning shoulder.

"Mmmmm, whassamatter?" Persia twisted her head and winced at the pain. She'd crooked her shoulders and the back of her neck by crawling around on her hands and knees all morning.

"Phone for you, honey—it's Marsh."

Pain was instantly forgotten as Persia flung off the sheet and sat up. "Marsh? Is he here? Is he coming back tonight?"

"Whoa! Wait and let me turn on a light, or you'll break your neck. My goodness, you don't fit that bed, do you? I should have given it to Chip, but then, with Ann and all—"

"Kathy, the phone?"

"Oh. Tom just talked to him, and now he wants to speak to you, so hurry up. It's long distance."

There wasn't time for constraint to grow. Kathy watched

from the top of the stairs as Persia raced down them. "Hey," she called softly. "You can take it in our room."

Persia didn't even bother to answer. By the light from the upstairs hall, she located the phone table and snatched up the receiver. Kathy's voice chimed in from the upstairs extension to tell them both good night, and then Persia was alone with him.

"Marsh?" Her voice sounded trembly. Her hands were clammy, and her heart was doing triple time.

"You sound half asleep. Sweetheart, I'm sorry to get you out of bed, but I couldn't go to sleep without hearing your voice first, I was afraid I'd gone off the deep end and imagined it all. You are there, aren't you?"

His voice sounded huskier than usual. She tried to picture him on the other end of the line. Had he got out of bed to call her? Was he wearing those rugby pants? Or nothing at all?"

"Persia, where are you?"

"I'm right here. Where are you? We sound like a couple of kids, don't we?" She laughed softly.

Marsh leaned back in the worn leather chair, extending his legs in front of him. He'd taken off his tie and jacket, but he still had on the slacks and shirt he'd worn to Anderson and Spartanburg. It was hot as the devil in town.

He savored the echo of her laugh. God, he could eat her with a spoon! His imagination amplified the sound of her breathing, and he held the phone tucked against his neck as if it were her face.

"I feel like a kid." He chuckled. "A two-hundred-year-old kid. I'm beat, honey. If I weren't, I sure as hell wouldn't be talking to you like this tonight. Are you wearing that pink thing with the lace on it?"

"It's tea rose, and no, I'm wearing my yellow one."

"Describe it to me," he commanded with rough gentleness.

Persia lowered herself to the edge of the chair and closed her eyes. "It has tiny lavender flowers embroidered under the bust, and it's long, and it—"

"Not bust—breasts. Tell me—does it hug your body up under your breasts like the pink—the tea rose one does? Does it cup your bottom when you walk? Is the neckline low enough and wide enough so that your—"

"Marsh! You're embarrassing me," Persia rebuked. She was growing acutely aware of her own body, so much so that her voice sounded breathless. "Where are you, anyway? When are you coming back? What time is it?"

"It's about one-thirty in the morning and I'm right here in Columbia, love, and if I thought I wouldn't wind up wrapped around a pine tree, I'd be on my way to Pinopolis right now. But it's been a hell of a day, and I'm not as young as I'd like to be."

"Marsh...I wish you were here," she confided with soft boldness.

He groaned. "Damn! Maybe I'm not as old as I thought I was. Do you have any idea what your voice and my imagination are doing to me right now?"

She giggled. "The same thing your voice and my imagination are doing to me, I hope."

"With a few minor variations. What did you do today?"

"I laid the brick you were going to help me with." After she'd decided not to run away like a scared chicken, that is. Good Lord, what if she had?

"You shouldn't wear yourself out that way. I want you nice and rested when I get there."

"Don't you think I should get all my work done so we can spend our time—fishing?"

"Fishing, hmmm? Interesting euphemism. I'll get my rod and tackle all ready. Reserve the float boat for us, will you? The Jon boat isn't roomy enough for what I have in mind."

All innocence, Persia crooned, "Oh? Were you planning on going after big game?"

"You guessed it," he retorted huskily. "And sweetheart—in case you're worried, I've got a fishing licence."

Sudden weakness assailed her. She clutched the phone and waited for it to pass. "Marsh—are you sure?"

"Honey, I can't go into it over the phone at this time of night. Just trust me. I've got to go to Hartsville and probably Florence, too, in the morning. I should be able to wind things up one way or another and be with you by the middle of the afternoon. If I manage to get a few hours sleep, that is. A cold shower is definitely indicated, but it's not going to help me get to sleep."

Several minutes later, Persia embraced her pillow and smiled herself to sleep.

She awakened early and hungry. Floating downstairs, she went straight for the cake stand; gingerbread, rich, moist and unexpectedly filled with coconut. Topping it with the last of the pineapple-cream custard, she sat down and began to eat. Dreamily, she savored each forkful as she tried to pierce the veil of space with her imagination.

Was he still asleep? Was he just waking up, throwing back the covers and stretching that lovely body of his like a long, sleek cat? Had he dreamed about her? Was he thinking of her right this minute?

She rinsed out her plate, totally unconscious of having consumed half her day's calorie requirements in one sitting. Dieting was the last thing on her mind; she was in love with the whole world today.

Eighty-five miles away, Marsh frowned at the spilled coffee grounds on the kitchen floor and hurriedly repacked his briefcase. He hoped his cleaning lady would forgive him this one time. If he was going to grab a bite of breakfast on the road and still get finished with all he had to do before lunch, he didn't have time to clean up.

* * *

Tom wandered out to watch Persia work when he came in from a predawn fishing trip. He offered to hand her bricks and to shovel sand on top of the finished part so that it could begin to work its way down into the cracks, but that was as far as his talents went.

"What did Marsh have to say last night?" he asked, leaning on the shovel after the first minute or two.

"You talked to him, too, didn't you?" She was reluctant to share; it was all too tremulously new. With her record for fantasizing, she couldn't trust herself not to have dreamed up the whole thing.

"He said he'd be back today. Minus Marilee."

Glancing over her shoulder, Persia was struck by the intensity of Tom's expression. Ordinarily the most laconic of men, he only got excited when he hooked into something unexpectedly large. "Is Kathy very disappointed?" she asked.

His bony shoulders lifted and fell. "Hope not. I think she was pretty disappointed the first few days when Marilee wasn't interested in sunbathing or swimming or girl talk. By now, I reckon she knows they don't have much in common anymore."

"I'm sorry," Persia murmured lamely, finishing off one walkway and brushing the sand from her knees. Three more to go and she'd be done.

"Don't be. I've discouraged that friendship, if you can call it a friendship, for years. I'm only glad Marsh finally came to his senses. I'd hate to think I was responsible for his being miserable the rest of his life—I introduced them, remember? But Kath's always thought so much of Marilee, I couldn't say anything."

Persia began to transfer a stack of bricks to the area where she'd be working next. She paused to look up curiously. Good old sleepy Tom—she might have known he wasn't as blind as he pretended. No wonder he was in demand as a trial lawyer. With his ability to dissimulate, he could disarm the devil.

"Have you been up to something, Thomas?" Her lips twitched in response to his self-deprecating grin.

"Nothing illegal—a little collusion, a diversionary tactic or two."

Persia's teasing retort was lost as Kathy called from the porch. "Telephone, Persia—it's a man."

By the time she'd flown up seven steps and through the kitchen, Persia realized it couldn't be Marsh. Kathy would have said so. "Hello?" she greeted breathlessly.

"Persia, it's Pat."

She dropped onto the chair like a lead balloon. "What's wrong? Has my house burned down? Has something happened to Meggie?"

"Darling, calm down, nothing's wrong. At least nothing that can't be made right—I hope. I'm in Charleston. Mother and I came down for a Historical Society conference, and Mother's in bed with hives. I kept telling her to stick to veal cutlets—these Charleston cooks disguise everything in so many sauces you can never tell what you're eating. Evidently she got hold of a bit of crab."

"I'm sorry to hear that. How sick is she? I'm afraid I don't know anything about hives."

'They're painful, but hardly dangerous. She's nicely settled in the home of a friend. I'm the one who needs you. I called Shamburg and got your number. From what I can tell, you're only twenty or thirty miles away. Can you meet me?"

Oh, God, what timing! If she'd had any doubts about her feelings for her ex-fiancé, this was the proof. "Pat, I can't. I—I'm in the middle of a project and I can't just walk out on it."

"Then tell me how to get there. Persia, I have to see you. *Please.*"

Biting her lip in annoyance, she heard herself agreeing. "Take 52 to Moncks Corner, get on 6 and watch for the sign to Pinopolis." She described the house and told him how to find it, and hung up.

Damn! She resented the interruption. She'd planned to work all morning and then bathe and get dressed in her black linen and be waiting on the shady side of the porch when Marsh arrived. She couldn't be certain his imagination hadn't elaborated on her attractions, trimming off a pound here and an inch or so there, and she didn't want him to come back to earth too quickly.

Still, whatever Pat had to say couldn't take long. And he'd been good to her—it wasn't his fault that his mama thought her only son should save himself for someone more influential.

She remembered the first time she'd visited Hickory Hill Farms. Pat had been grooming his favorite show jumper. Slender, of moderate height, he'd been dressed in jodhpurs, gleaming black boots, and a yellow turtleneck sweater. Over the next few years, he'd taught her to ride, taught her to appreciate every mellow, historic old brick in the town of Fredericksburg, and taught her to value herself as an attractive woman. For that last, at least, she owed him a lot. Perhaps she even owed him her happiness.

She was still in her work clothes when he drove up. Hearing a car, she dusted the sand from her hands and knees and strolled around the corner of the house.

"Hi, Pat. How's your mother?"

"Persia? What happened to you?"

Oh, Lord, she'd forgotten. Pat had never seen her in the throes of a project before. She'd always taken great pains to spare him that. Megan was the slob of the family—Pat and his mother were equally fastidious.

She explained about the half-finished patio, and all the while her eyes were taking in the sight of Patrick in blue jeans and a T-shirt. Granted, the shirt was pristine white, with a discreet logo on the pocket, and the jeans were brand new and nicely creased, but it was still a Patrick she'd never seen before.

"Could we go somewhere and talk?" he asked.

"How about the screened porch. It's the coolest place I know—I'll get us some iced tea."

"Never mind that—I have to get back pretty soon in case mother needs something. Persia, would you—could you...well, I think I might have been a bit hasty."

She led him inside. Seated on the glider, she let her eyes roam over his dark-lashed blue eyes and his neatly groomed black hair, and found herself totally unaffected by his aristocratic good looks. She listened while he hesitantly admitted that he'd missed her and hoped they could see something of each other when she went back home.

Before he could elaborate, she broke in gently. "Pat, no. You were absolutely right about us—we'd have been awful together. I'd have had to be on my best behavior, and I can only play lady so long without getting cramps in my psyche. Your mother's right—you need a wife who can fit into your lifestyle better. I might have managed it once, a long time ago, but it wouldn't have lasted. I'd rather spend my time digging in compost than pouring tea and running worthy organizations.

Kathy opened the front door and peered through the screen. "Persia? Did I hear voices out here?"

Persia introduced them, chaffing at the delay. She'd wanted to finish one more section of bricks before she stopped to shower and change. There was always a chance that Marsh might get through earlier than he'd expected, and this time she wasn't going to be caught unprepared.

"You'll have to meet my husband, Tom—he's a lawyer, too. Why don't you stay to lunch, Patrick? We'd love to have you, wouldn't we, Persia?"

No, we would not, Persia thought grimly. "Pat has to get back to Charleston. His mother's allergic to crabs."

"But you can't leave without meeting Tom—y'all are both lawyers. You'll have lots of things in common. Now, you wait right here, all right?" Kathy disappeared to go find Tom, and Persia stood up and edged toward the door. If Tom wanted to get met, he'd better hurry, because she was about to forget her manners and hurry Pat on his way.

They were still on the porch, with Persia practically chewing her nails in frustration, when Marsh drove up. He parked in the shade of one of the huge magnolias that dotted the yard, and she broke off in mid-sentence and waited for him to get out of the car. She was starved for a glimpse of him!

Marsh rubbed a hand tiredly across the back of his neck and whistled a sigh through his teeth. Who the devil was that pretty-boy on the front porch? A traveling salesman? No—not if he belonged to the black Seville in the middle of the driveway. Damn it, he'd burned up the highway getting here. Maybe he didn't expect her to come flying out to meet him, but at least he hadn't expected her to be tied up with some other man.

Cool it, Randolph—her name might be Persia, but she's not in purdah. It was probably just a neighbor looking for Tom. He opened the door and felt a bead of perspiration trickle down his stomach.

"Is this your cousin's husband?" Patrick inquired.

Marsh sized up the younger man in one swift, hooded glance. With gut certainty, he identified him: that damned Virginian of hers.

Persia made the introductions, and Marsh forced himself to be civil. He had half a mind to sweep her into his arms and kiss the living daylights out of her, but to do it, he'd have to pass that limp, pale hand.

Reluctantly, he shook it and dropped it. "Blake," he acknowledged curtly. "Just passing through?"

"Actually, I'm staying in Charleston for a few more days. I came by to see Persia, and her cousin was good enough to invite me to lunch. You're visiting here, too?"

Marsh nodded briefly. His every instinct told him the man was no real threat, but he had too much at stake to take any chances now. If she'd been the one to break off the engagement, he'd have felt safer—as it was, she might be still harboring some vestige of feeling for him. He was a smooth customer, all right.

"I believe Persia mentioned that you're a lawyer, too," Patrick probed, his eyes cool and watchful.

"No, that's Tom—my cousin's husband," Persia broke in, determined to set the record straight and then get rid of Patrick. This was *not* the way she'd envisioned Marsh's homecoming. "Marsh owns newspapers. Weeklies. In three states," she said shortly. *There's nothing for you here,* she wanted to add, *so why don't you leave?*

She might have known it wouldn't be that easy. Standing by helplessly, she heard Pat's cultivated voice sound out the depth of Marsh's influence. A budding politician needed all the press he could get.

"Look, you all, if you'll excuse me, I'll just go in and see if I can lend Kathy a hand with lunch. Come on inside in a few minutes, all right?" Her eyes pleaded with Marsh to understand, but she couldn't tell whether he got the message or not. He and Pat were standing there bristling like a pair of cur dogs, and there wasn't a blessed thing she could do about it.

She let herself inside. "Kathy? Tom?" She called out softly.

"Understand you have a gentleman caller," Tom said, sauntering in from the back of the house. "Kath said he's staying for lunch."

"Oh, Tom, I'm so mad I could spit nails!" Persia whispered. "It's Patrick—my ex-fiancé. He would have to show up now, of all times, just when Marsh—" She broke off abruptly. Just how much Tom knew about what had been going on this past week, she wasn't sure. Giving him credit for more astuteness than was apparent on the surface, she confided in him.

"Remember, now—give me half an hour to shower and get ready, then send Marsh down to the boat," she said urgently a few minutes later. "I don't care what you do with Pat, as long as you keep him away."

"Trust me. You say the fellow raises horses? Don't know a damned thing about the creatures myself, but I can ask enough questions to keep him talking till suppertime."

"Oh, please—just feed him and get rid of him, will you? He's really sweet as pie," she called over her shoulder as she took the steps two at a time. "You'll adore each other!"

Trusting that Marsh wasn't watching from the house, Persia lowered the furled sun-shade on the side of the float boat so that she wouldn't be so readily visible from the pier. Before boarding, she fixed the lines so that she could release them with a flip and be off.

It was childish, silly, ridiculous! She settled herself on the far side, arranging her legs in a position that showed off their golden length to the best advantage. Marsh would probably laugh himself silly! As second thoughts undermined her courage, she clapped her hand on her hat and jumped up again. If only Tom would keep him occupied five minutes longer, she could sneak inside and change into something more appropriate than the black linen dress.

Too late. He was almost at the pier. The sight of those long, lean, khaki-clad legs and the soft, vanilla-colored deck shoes brought a hollow feeling to the pit of her stomach. From the shelter of the concealing awning, she watched his approach. He wasn't wearing any socks, but then that didn't mean anything—he never did with deck shoes. It was too late to back out now, anyway.

"Persia, honey? You aboard? Shall I cast off?"

Oh, no—she'd meant to have a bottle of wine and two glasses. They'd die of thirst! "No! I mean—just get on board, will you?"

In one smooth movement he swung himself under the canopy, a quizzical expression on his face. "Why do I get the feeling I've done something wrong?"

Flinging the ridiculously romantic leghorn hat from her head, she sat up and glared at him. "It's not you—it's me!" Her scowl faltered as she saw him put down the brown paper bag he'd been carrying. "What's that?"

"If I'm going to be shanghaied, I thought I'd do it in style. Do you mind?"

"Did Tom tell you what was going on?" she demanded suspiciously. The sun was beating fiercely down on her back, and she could feel perspiration gathering in the valley of her spine. Black linen was damnably hot—even with nothing under it.

Marsh leaned forward and flipped the bowline from the cleat; moving aft, he cast off the stern line, and shoved them away from the pier. "Shall I start the motor, or do we just sail silently off into the sunset?"

"We use the motor. It's faster." Her doubt-induced irritation was beginning to fade under the balm of his teasing eyes. "It's cooler, too. I thought you'd be getting back later on, when it wasn't so hot. And then Pat showed up, and I had to revise my plans."

Starting the motor, he headed them away from land. "Blame my impetuous nature, honey. I rushed through everything so fast this morning I didn't have time to warn you. I like your dress, by the way. Is that the latest in yachting attire?''

Persia looked down at the disgracefully expensive simplicity. It flattered what it covered, and it exposed large amounts of golden brown flesh, both above and below. She eased off one of her sandals, a matter of three straps and a four inch heel. ''No, it's just a sample of how practical I can be when I put my mind to it. Marsh, if you're smart, you'll go over the side and start swimming right now, and not look back.''

There was a gentle knowingness about him—a certain curve of his lips, a special glow in his eyes. He saw right through her. She sighed and slipped off the other shoe. ''Marsh, are you sure you don't want to back out of this business? You see the sort of thing I'm capable of…I get these bizarre ideas, and before I know it, I'm doing something utterly foolish. I was going to be so cool and glamorous and seductive, and instead I'm hot and sticky and thirsty, and I forgot to bring the wine.''

Marsh nodded to the brown paper bag that was sitting upright halfway between them. ''I remembered.''

''Whose fantasy is this, anyhow?''

''Ours?'' he offered tentatively. ''The bottle's in a wine brick. How about wetting it down again and sitting it in the shade while I put some distance between you and that baby-faced lawyer of yours, will you?''

She ignored the crack about Patrick. Glad to be doing something sensible for a change, she opened the bag and took out the bisque cylinder. There were two carefully wrapped glasses and a rectangular package wrapped in foil. She took them all out. Scooping up lake water in one of the glasses, she poured it down the sides of the cooler so that evaporation would cool the bottle inside.

''What's in the box?''

''Your engagement present.''

Her heart beat wildly. She couldn't think of a single thing to say.

"You can open it once we reach our cove and drop anchor," he told her. "I'll help you with it."

They passed two boatloads of teenagers and several anchored fisherman. By the time they reached the relatively secluded arm of the lake where they'd made love, Persia was sure she was getting seasick. She swallowed convulsively as Marsh eased the anchor over the side. "Could I have a sip of wine first?" she whispered.

"Sure, honey—anything you want." He peeled his shirt over his head and began to step out of his khakis. Persia was relieved to see that he was wearing trunks underneath. And then she cried out softly, "Oh, no!"

"What's wrong?"

"I forgot my bathing suit," she wailed. Nothing was going the way she'd planned it! The plain truth was, her great seduction scene might have been perfect for a moon-lit night, but for high noon on a crowded lake, it was nothing short of ludicrous. Not to mention inconvenient. And embarrassing.

"It didn't bother you the last time," he reminded her, reaching for the wine. He poured two glasses and handed her one. "Drink up and forget your inhibitions, love. If it will help, I'll take off my trunks."

"Don't you dare!" She took a large gulp of her wine and almost strangled. When she'd recovered, she set the glass aside, and her eyes returned to the glittering box on the console.

"Curious?" he taunted.

"Not really," Persia replied with feigned coolness. "But if you don't open it right now you're going to be in serious trouble. I'm not the patient sort."

He laughed and reached for the mysterious package. "I forgot and left your ring in my jacket. It's nothing fancy,

I'm afraid. I thought something simple—a wide, all-purpose band that would fit under gardening gloves—would be better, but if you'd rather have a—"

"Marsh, are you really going to marry me?" she blurted, clutching his arm. He hadn't even kissed her yet, and here she was practically engaged.

"Just as fast as the law allows, sweetheart," he murmured. "And in South Carolina, they're pretty efficient about that sort of thing." His eyes caressed every visible inch of her as he slowly unwrapped the box. When he heard her gasp of disbelief, he laughed aloud. "Disappointed?"

"Marsh, I can't believe it! Do you realize that no one's *ever* given me chocolates before? I guess they thought it was tactless or something—I—oh, darling, I don't know what to say! Thank you, thank you." She leaned forward and aimed a kiss at his mouth, and it landed on his chin. The five-pound box of cherry cordials and all the wrappings were between them on the padded seat.

"You can do better than that. Shall we sample one first?" He took out one of the dark chocolates and held it for her to bite.

"The juice will drip out," she protested, laughing.

"Don't worry about it," he murmured, watching as she sank her teeth into the rich confection. He tilted it quickly to cup the remaining liqueur as he carried it to his own lips. And then he reached out and lifted her to her feet, enclosing her in his arms as he mingled his sweetness with hers. "Share and share alike, I always say," he whispered a long time later.

"Marsh, you can't indulge me this way, you know. One of these days I'll get too fat to make love."

"And one of these days I'll get too old. So we'll spend our twilight years fishing."

"I adore the way you fish," she growled, sliding her

hands under the top of his trunks to stroke the cool flesh of his hips.

"I'm not sure I can wait for it to grow dark. Maybe if we hang out a yellow fever flag to warn off other mariners...?"

"Sorry—fresh out of flags. We could let down the sides."

"And suffocate. What I have in mind requires a certain amount of exertion."

"We could always pass a little time by talking first," she suggested. They could do anything, as long as they did it together. The pleasure she got from merely being in his presence was more intense than anything she'd ever experienced with another man. If it got any sweeter, she might die from an overload of happiness.

"That's not exactly what I had in mind, but if you think you can talk and make love at the same time, help yourself." His fingers had found the hidden zipper at her back, and he was lowering it with tantalizing slowness. "You're not wearing a bra," he observed.

"I'm not wearing a lot of things. Marsh, where will we live? Your place or mine?" She reached up and traced the hairline at his temple, and then began to explore the shape of his ear.

"I can relocate my office, I guess, since you own your own home. I've spent a lot of time on the road, but I can probably organize things so that I can operate from a central location."

"I wouldn't mind moving back home again to South Carolina. What's your place like?" She glanced quickly at the half-lowered sun-shade as Marsh peeled off the top of her dress.

"Not even a window box, I'm afraid." He began to kiss the side of her throat, and then he cupped his hands beneath her breasts and continued his caresses until she caught her breath sharply.

"Marsh, I can't concentrate when you do that."

"No?" His hands slipped inside her skirt and rounded her buttocks, pulling her hard against him. "Does this help?"

She cast a frantic glance over his shoulder, seeing several fishing boats, but none close by. Her relief was shattered by another concern. "Marsh, my chocolates are melting!"

He laughed. "Beloved, so am I, in case you hadn't noticed." He stepped back, allowing his hands to fall away from her. Sliding the box in the shade, he spread the reflective foil over the top. "I'll buy you all the chocolates you want, sweetheart."

"You'll do no such thing, Marsh Randolph. You'll feed me raw spinach and broccoli and broiled chicken."

"I want to give you pleasure. I want to spoil you," he whispered, drawing her over to the side of the boat that faced the secluded shore. He slid her dress down over her hips and held it while she stepped out of it. "And I want you to pleasure me and spoil me. Starting now. Over we go."

The water was cool, stimulating to the skin, and incredibly sensuous as it swirled around them. They went under together, laughter bubbling up above them as Persia executed an uninhibited underwater dance. He caught her and she surfaced in his arms, exhilarated with the sheer intensity of her emotions.

"Have you got some sort of hangup about making love in a bed?" she taunted, holding his hands and floating up until her backside broke the surface and bobbed there.

"If the bed's five feet long and three feet wide, I have." He drifted up and captured her waist with his feet.

"Marsh, do you know what stretch marks are? I have seven of them. Maybe you'd better look."

"Honey, don't distract me with nonessentials. I've been planning this scene since I hung up the phone just before two this morning."

"*You've* been planning it! This is *my* fantasy!"

"I told you my motto—share and share alike."

With a deft maneuver, he rearranged their relative positions more to his liking.

It was to Persia's liking, as well. Intensely so.

* * * * *

American HEROES
AGAINST ALL ODDS

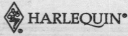

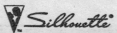

Please address questions and book requests to: Harlequin Reader Service U.S.: 3010 Walden Ave.,
P.O. Box 1325, Buffalo, NY 14269 CAN.: P.O. Box 609, Fort Erie, Ont. L2A 5X3   PAHGEN

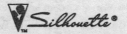

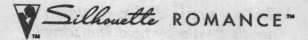